A CAPILLARY CRIME

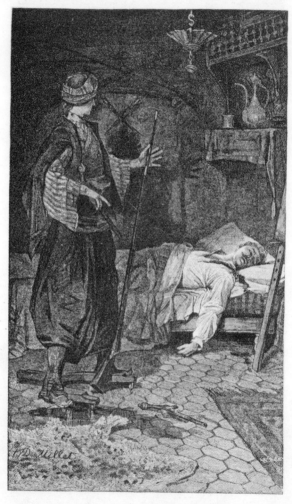

APPEARANCE OF MANDEL'S STUDIO THE MORNING AFTER
HIS DEATH.

A CAPILLARY CRIME

AND OTHER STORIES

BY

FRANCIS D. MILLET

ILLUSTRATED

Short Story Index Reprint Series

BOOKS FOR LIBRARIES PRESS
FREEPORT, NEW YORK

PS2399
M68C3

First Published 1892
Reprinted 1971

INTERNATIONAL STANDARD BOOK NUMBER:
0-8369-3905-0

LIBRARY OF CONGRESS CATALOG CARD NUMBER:
72-157793

PRINTED IN THE UNITED STATES OF AMERICA

CONTENTS.

A CAPILLARY CRIME

A CAPILLARY CRIME

NEAR the summit of the hill in the
Quartier Montmartre, Paris, is a little
street in which the grass grows between
the paving-stones, as in the avenues of
some dead old Italian city. Tall buildings
border it for about one third its length,
and the walls of tiny gardens, belonging to
houses on adjacent streets, occupy the rest
of its extent. It is a populous thorough-
fare, but no wheels pass through it, for the
very good reason that near the upper end
it suddenly takes a short turn, and shoots
up the hill at an incline too steep for a
horse to climb. The regular morning refuse
cart, and on rare occasions a public carriage,
venture a short distance into the lower part
of the street, and even these, on wet, slippery days, do not pass the door of the first

house. Scarcely two minutes' walk from the
busy exterior boulevards, this little corner
of the great city is as quiet as a village nearly all day long. Early in the morning the
sidewalks clatter with the shoes of workmen
hurrying down to their work, children scam-
per along playing hide-and-seek in the door-
ways on their way to school, and then follows
a long silence, broken only by the glazier
with his shrill cry, "Vi-i-i-tri-er!" or the farmer with his "À la crème, fromage à la crème!"
In the late summer afternoons the women
bring their babies out and sit on the door-
steps, as the Italians do, gossiping across the
street, and watching the urchins pitch sous
against the curb-stone, or draw schoolboy
hieroglyphics on the garden walls. There is
a musical quiet in this little street. Birds
sing merrily in the stunted trees of the shady
gardens, the familiar calls of hens and chick-
ens and the shrill crows of the cock come
from every enclosure, and all the while is
heard the deep and continuous note of the
rumble of the city down below. At night
the street is lighted by two lanterns swung

on ropes between opposite houses; and the flickering, dim light, sending uncertain shadows upon the blank walls and the towering façades, gives the place a weird and fantastic aspect.

Montmartre is full of these curious highways. Quite distinct from the rest of the city by reason of its elevated position, few or no modern improvements have changed its character, and a large extent of it remains to-day much the same as it was fifty years ago.

It is perhaps the cheapest quarter of the city. Rents are low, and the necessities and commodities of life are proportionately cheaper than in other parts of the town. This fact, and the situation the quarter affords for unobstructed view of the sky, have always attracted artists, and many cosy studios are hidden away in the maze of housetops there. On the little street I have just described are several large windows indicating unmistakably the profession of those occupying the apartments.

Late one dark and stormy evening a gate

creaked and an automatic bell sounded at
the entrance to one of the little gardens half-
way up the street. A young woman came
out into the light of the swinging lantern,
and hurried down the sidewalk. Her un-
naturally quick and spasmodic movements
showed she was anxious to get away from
the neighborhood as quickly as possible.
Her instinctive avoidance of the bad places
in the sidewalk gave evidence of her famil-
iarity with the locality. In a few moments
she had left the tortuous narrow side street
that led down the hill, and stood upon the
brilliantly lighted boulevard. Pausing for
an instant only, she rapidly crossed the
street, and soon stood beside the fountain
in the Place Pigalle. Here she watched for
a moment the surface of the water, ruffled
by the gusts of wind and beaten by the
fierce rain-drops. Suddenly she turned and
hurried away down the Rue Pigalle, across
to the Rue Blanche, and was shortly lost in
the crowd that was pouring out of the doorway of the skating-rink.

The little street on the hill remained deserted and desolate. The lights in the windows went out one by one. The wind gusts swayed the lanterns to and fro, creaking the rusty pulleys and rattling the glass in the iron frames. Now and then a gate was blown backward and forward with a dull sound, a shutter slammed, and between the surges of the wind could be heard the spirting of the stream from the spouts and the rush of the water in the gutters. Towards midnight a single workman staggered up the street from the cheap cabaret kept in the wood-and-charcoal shop on the corner. A little later a *sergent de ville*, wrapped in a cloak, passed slowly up the sidewalk, until he came to a spot where the asphalt was worn away, and there was a great pool of muddy water. There he stopped, turned around, and strode down the street again. The melancholy music of the storm went on.

Suddenly, towards morning, there was a dull, prolonged report like the sound of a distant blast of rocks. The great studio window over the little garden flashed red

for an instant, then grew black again, and
all was still. Away up on the opposite side
of the street a window was opened, a head
thrust out, and, meeting the drenching rain,
was quickly withdrawn. A hand and bare
arm were pushed through the half-open window, feeling for the fastening of the shutter. In an adjoining house a light was seen
in the window, and it continued to burn.
Then the mournful music of the tempest
went on as before.

Shortly after daybreak the same young
woman who had fled so hastily the evening
before, slowly and with difficulty mounted the
hill. Her clothes were saturated with the
rain, and clung to her form as the violent
wind caught her and sent her staggering
along. Her bonnet was out of shape and
beaten down around her ears, and her dark
hair was matted on her forehead. Her face
was haggard, and her eyes were large and
full of a strange gleam. She was evidently
of Southern birth, for her features had the
sculpturesque regularity of the Italian, and
her skin, though pallid and bloodless, was

still deep in tone. She hesitated at the garden gate for a while, then opened it, entered, and shut it behind her, the automatic bell tinkling loudly. No one appearing at the door, she opened and shut the gate again to ring the bell. A second and third time she rang in the same way, and without any response from the house. At last, hearing no sound, she crossed the garden, tried the house door, and, finding it unlocked, opened it and went in. Shortly afterwards a frightened cry was heard in the studio, and a moment later the girl came out of the house, her haggard face white with fear. Clutching her hands together with a nervous motion, she hastened down the street. A half-hour later a *femme de ménage* opened the gate, passed through the garden, and tried her key in the door. Finding it unlocked, she simply said, " Perhaps he's gone out," and went into the kitchen and began to prepare breakfast. Before the water boiled the gate opened sharply, and three persons entered; first, the martial figure of a *sergent de ville;* second, a tall, blond young man in a brown

velveteen coat and waistcoat and light trousers ; and, lastly, the girl, still trembling and
panting. The *sergent* carefully locked the
gate on the inside, taking the key with him,
and, followed by the young man, entered
the house, paused in the kitchen for a few
rapid words with the *femme de ménage*, and
then went up into the studio. The girl
crouched down upon the stone step by the
gate and hid her face.

The studio was of irregular shape, having
curious projections and corners, and one third
of the ceiling lower than the rest. The alcove
formed by this drop in the ceiling was about
the size of an ordinary bedchamber. The
drawn curtain of the large side window shut
out so much of the dim daylight that the
whole studio was in twilight. In the farther
corner of the deep alcove was a low divan,
filling the recess between a quaint staircase
which led into the attic and the wall opposite
the window. This divan served as a bed,
and on it, half covered with the bedclothes,
lay a man, stretched on his back, with his
face turned towards the window. The left

arm hung over the edge of the divan, and
the hand, turned inertly under the wrist,
rested on the floor.   There was the unmis-
takable pallor of death on the face, visible
even in the uncertain gloom.   The *sergent*
quickly lowered the curtain, letting in a flood
of cold, gray light.   Then great blood-stains
were seen on the pillow, and on the neck
and shoulders of the shirt.   Beside the bed
stood, like a grim guard of the dead body,
the rigid and angular figure of a manikin
dressed in Turkish costume.   Between the
manikin and the window lay on the floor a
large flint-lock pistol.   Near the window
stood an easel, with a large canvas turned
away from the light.

The two men paused in the middle of the
studio, and looked at the spectacle without
speaking.   Then the young man rushed to
the divan, and caught the arm that hung
over the side, but dropped it instantly again.

"Touch nothing.   Do not touch a single
object," commanded the *sergent*, sternly.
Then he approached the body himself, put
his hand on the face, and said, "He is dead."

Taking the young man by the arm, he led him out of the room, carefully locking the door behind him. In the kitchen he wrote a few words on a leaf torn from his note-book, gave it to the *femme de ménage* with a ·hasty direction, checked her avalanche of questions with a single, significant gesture, led the way into the garden, unlocked the gate, and half pushed her into the street.

He stood quietly watching the crouching figure of the young girl for some time, then stooping over her, raised her, half forcibly, half gently, to her feet, and pointed out that the place where she sat was wet and muddy. Then he made a few commonplace remarks about the weather. In a short time the *femme de ménage* returned, breathless, ac-companied by two more officers, one of them a lieutenant.

It was curious to see the instantaneous transformation of the little street when the *femme de ménage* and the two policemen entered the gate. Windows were opened and heads thrust out on all sides. It was impossible to say where the people came

from, but in a very short time the street was
blocked with a crowd that gathered around
the gate. Those on the sidewalk struggled
to get a peep through the gate, while those
in the street stared fixedly at the studio
window. One or two tried to force the gate
open, but a *sergent de ville*, posted inside,
pushed the bolts in place. The *femme de
ménage*, who had managed to get a glimpse
of the scene in the studio, sat weeping dra-
matically at the kitchen window.

The lieutenant and the *sergent* who first
came went from one room to another, examining everything with care, to see if there
had been a robbery. In the studio they
scrutinized every inch of the room, even to
the dust-covered stairway that led to the little attic over the alcove. Then, after a hasty
examination of the corpse, they mounted the
stairway that led from the entry to the roof,
and searched for fresh scratches on the lead-
covered promenade there. Apparently satisfied with the completeness of their search,
they remained awhile there, looking at the
slated roof, and at the hawthorn-tree which

stretched two or three strong branches almost up to the iron railing of the balcony.

The lieutenant then, with great deliberation, took down in his note-book the exact
situation in the studio, measuring carefully
the distance of the pistol from the body,
noting the angle of the wound (for the ball
had gone through the head just over the ear),
taking account of many things that would
have escaped the attention of the ordinary
observer. When this was finished, he sent
away one of the *sergents*, who shortly returned with two men bearing a stretcher, or
rather a rusty black bier. The men were
conducted to the studio, and there, with
business-like haste, they placed the body on
the bier, strapped it firmly there, covered it
with a soiled and much-worn black cloth,
and with the aid of the officers carried it
down the stairs and out of the house into
the garden. The girl, who had remained
standing where the *sergent* had placed her,
sank down again on the stone steps at the
sight of the black bier and its burden, and
hid her face in her hands. There was a

momentary gleam of something like satisfaction in the eye of the *sergent* who stood be
side her.

The lieutenant, who had remained to put
seals on the door of the studio, on the door
which led out upon the promenade, and
upon all the windows of the upper stories,
came out of the house, followed by the
young man in the velveteen coat, and the
weeping *femme de ménage*. The lieutenant
had a bundle in his arms a foot and a half
long, done up in a newspaper. He gave the
sergent at the gate a brief order, then went
out into the street, clearing the sidewalk of
the crowd. The body was next borne out,
and the young man and the two women, followed by one of the *sergents*, presented
themselves to the eyes of the curious multitude. Without delay the two bearers
marched off down the street at a rapid pace,
the heavy burden shaking with the rhythm
of their step. The little procession of officers and prisoners, accompanied by the
whole of the great crowd, followed the bier
to the prefecture. There a preliminary ex-

amination of the two women and the young
man was held, and they were all detained as
witnesses. The body was carried to the
morgue.

It would be tedious to describe in detail
the different processes of law which to our
Anglo-Saxon eyes appear but empty and
useless indignities heaped upon the defence-
less dead. Neither would it be an attractive
task to give a minute account of the meagre
funeral ceremonies which the friends of the
dead artist conducted, after they had succeeded in getting possession of the body for
burial. The grave was dug in the cemetery
of Montmartre, and the few simple tributes
of friendship placed on the mound were lost
among the flashing filigree emblems and
gaudy wreaths which adorned the surround-
ing tombstones.

The theories which were advanced by the
three officers who had examined the prem-
ises were distinguished by some invention
and ingenuity. From carefully collected information concerning the intimate life and
whole history of the three persons kept as

witnesses, the officers constructed each his separate romance about the motives for the crime and the manner in which it was committed. The lieutenant had quite a voluminous biography of each character.

Concerning Charles Mandel, the dead artist, it was found that he was a native of Styria, in Austria; that his parents and all his relatives were exceedingly poor; that he had worked his way up from a place as a farmer's boy to a position as attendant in the baths at Gastein, and thence he had found his way to Munich, and to the School of Fine Arts there. He had taken a good rank in the Academy, and after several years' study, supporting himself meanwhile on a small government subsidy and by the sale of pen-and-ink sketches, he began to paint pictures. When he had saved money enough he came to Paris, where he had lived about eighteen months. His character was unimpeachable. He lived quietly, and rarely went out of the quarter; was never seen at the balls in the old windmill on the summit of Montmartre, nor did he frequent the

2

Élisée Montmartre, the skating rink, the Cirque Fernando, nor any other place of amusement in the neighborhood. The little Café du Rat Mort, in the Place Pigalle, was the only café he visited, and in this he was accustomed to pass an hour or two every evening in company with his friend, the sculptor Paul Benner. He was not known to have any enemies, there was no suspicion that he was connected with the International-alists, and the only reason he had been re-marked at all as an individual was because he spoke French badly, and always con-versed in German with his friend Benner.

The information concerning the latter was a great deal more accurate and precise. A great deal of it, however, was irrelevant. He was born in Strasburg, in 1849, and be-gan the study of his profession there. He came to Paris when he was twenty years old, and entered the Académie des Beaux Arts. After he had finished the course he set up his studio in Montmartre, and had already exhibited successful works in three *salons*. He had a great many friends in the city, and

was well spoken of by all who knew him.
The only thing that could possibly be urged
against him was the fact that he seemed
very little disturbed at the idea of being a
Prussian subject. But he was consistently
cosmopolitan, as his intimate friendship with
the Austrian and his equally close relations
with fellow-students in the Beaux Arts abun-
dantly proved.

The inquiries about the girl were, judging
from the frequent gaps in the history as
written in the lieutenant's note-book, conducted with difficulty, and with only partial
success. She was a Corsican, and was generally called Rose Blanche, the translation of
her Corsican name, Rosina Bianchi. By the
artists she was facetiously called La Rose
Blanche, partly because of her hair and complexion, which were of the darkest Southern
hue, and partly for the sake of the gram-
matical harmony of the name thus altered.
Nothing in particular was found out about
her early life. She herself declared she was
born in a small village in the mountains of
Corsica, and that her father, mother, and

several brothers and sisters were still living there. She had come to Paris as a model just before the siege, having first begun to pose in Marseilles, whither she had gone from Corsica to live with an aunt. This aunt had married a crockery merchant, and was a respectable member of the community. From her was gleaned some notion of the family. It was of genuine Corsican stock, and they all had the violent passions which are the common characteristic of that people. Rosina, while in Marseilles, had been quiet and proper enough except when she had been, as her aunt described, *un peu toquee*. At long intervals it seems that she became highly sensitive and excitable. She would on these occasions fly into a mad rage at a trifle, and when she grew calmer would sob and weep for a while, and end by remaining sullen and morose for hours, sometimes for days. Her aunt had opposed her going to Paris, prophesying all sorts of evil. She had never seen her since her departure, and had only heard from her twice or three times since she had left Marseilles.

There was scarcely a better-known model in Paris than La Rose Blanche. She was not one of those choice favorites who are engaged for months and sometimes for a year in advance at double prices, but she was in great demand, especially among sculptors. Her head was Italian enough to serve as a model for the costume pictures of the Campagna peasants, but she was much more picturesque as a Spanish girl, and her employment among the painters was chiefly with those who painted Spanish or Eastern subjects. The sculptors found in her form a certain girlishness which had not disappeared with age, and although she was twenty-five years old, she had the lithe, slender figure of a girl of seventeen. There was something of the faun in the accents of her limbs, and she was active, wiry, and muscular. The artists connected the peculiarities of her figure with the characteristics of her disposition, and often said to her, " What a hand and arm for a stiletto !" "Yes," she would answer, with a glittering eye ; " and it isn't afraid to hold one either !" Every one had noticed her violent temper, and some of those who were best acquainted with her confessed to the feeling that it was like playing with gunpowder to have much to do with her. When she was in good spirits, she was soft-mannered and amiable; but when roused in the least, she became like a fury. She had frequently posed in the *ateliers*, and then she had been treated with great respect by the students. For the past year she had served often as a model for Benner in the execution of his statue "Diana surprised at her Bath," and when she was not at work with him was generally in Mandel's studio, where she posed for a figure in a picture from the history of Hungary, an event in one of the Turkish invasions. With the exception of the report of her eccentricities of temper, nothing had counted against her. Even this was partly counterbalanced by the testimony of many to whom she had been both kind and useful. As far as her moral character went, some had said, with an expressive shrug of the shoulders, " She's a model, and like all the rest of them." Others had declared that she was undoubtedly honest and virtuous. No one knew anything—at least no one confessed to any positive knowledge—of her suspected transgressions.

The poor *femme de ménage*, whose life had been hitherto without an event worth the attention of the police, did not escape the most rigid scrutiny. Her history was sifted out as carefully as that of the other three. She was married to a second husband, and the mother of a boy of eighteen, who was salesman in one of the large dry-goods shops. Her husband, besides the duties of concierge in the house where they lived—an occupation which paid for the rent of the rooms they occupied—managed to make a trifle at his trade of tailor, repairing and turning old garments, and on rare occasions making a new coat or a pair of trousers for an old customer. He was also employed as a supernumerary in the Grand Opera, a duty which obliged him to attend the theatre often, to the serious interruption of his home occupations. He could not well give up the

place in the theatre, for his salary was just
enough, with the rest he earned, to make
both ends meet. The wife was obliged to
be at home so much, to fill her husband's
place in the care of the great house, that she
could only manage to do very little outside
work. The families in the house were all
working people, and consequently could not
afford the luxury of assistance in the kitchen.
She therefore found a place as *femme de
ménage* with some family in the vicinity.
For some time she had been in the employ of
the dead artist, and was particularly satisfied
with the place, first because she could choose
her own hours, and then because she had
very little to do, and was paid as much as if
she took care of a family—twenty francs a
month. One circumstance excited the suspicion of the police. She had been gone
nearly the whole afternoon of the day before
the murder. When she returned at dark her
husband noticed that she was heated and
confused, and asked her where she had been.
She refused to tell him, painfully trying to
make the refusal palatable by jokes. And

the police with little difficulty found out exactly what she had been doing for the three
or four hours in question. She had been to
the Cemetery of Montmartre. She had been
seen by the keepers there busy near a grave
on the third side avenue to the left, about a
quarter way up the slope. They had observed her digging up the two small flower-
ing shrubs she had planted there years before, and had constantly tended. These
shrubs she had wrapped up in an old colored
shirt, and had carried them away. Further,
a neighbor of the dead artist in the little
street on Montmartre deposed that late in
the afternoon of the day before the tragedy
she had seen the *femme de ménage* enter the
gate of the studio garden, bearing an irreg-
ular-shaped bundle of considerable size.
The police, on visiting the garden, found the
two shrubs described by the keepers of the
cemetery freshly planted in the little central
plot.

Then for the first time they questioned
the *femme de ménage* herself, and she confessed, with an abundance of tears, that her

only daughter had died five years previous, and that she had been buried in the Cimetière Montmartre, and the grave had been purchased for the period of five years. The term was to expire within a few days, and the poor woman, unable to pay for a further lease of ground, was obliged to give up her claim to the grave. She could not bear to lose the shrubs, for they were souvenirs of her dead child, who cultivated them when very small plants in flower-pots on the balcony. The mother had dug them up in the cemetery, and transplanted them in the garden of the house where she worked, having no garden-plot of her own. She intended the next day to tell the artist what she had done, and to get his permission to let the shrubs flourish there. She had refused to explain her absence to her husband because the girl had been dead a year when she married him, and he had sometimes reproached her for spending her time in the cemetery. As it was not his child, he could not be expected to care for it; and the poor mother, not having the courage to ask for money to renew the lease of the grave, kept her own counsel about the matter.

The examination of the witnesses, and the investigation of their personal history, threw but little light upon the exact state of the relations which existed between the painter and La Rose Blanche. The neighbors had overheard at various times loud talking in the studio, and occasionally some violent language that sounded very much like a quarrel. One or two of the shrewd ones, especially an old woman who sold vegetables from a little hand-cart on the corner, volunteered their opinion that the model was in love with the artist. The withered and blear-eyed old huckster gave as reason for her opinion that the model had generally stayed long after painting hours, and was unusually prompt in the morning. But there was quite as much proof that Mandel did not care for the model as that she was enamoured of him. He never watched for her in the morning, never came to the door with her; treated her always, as far as was noticed by any one who had seen them together, as if on the most formal terms with her. In the Café du Rat Mort it was found that La Rose Blanche had often come in during the evening, sometimes in fine costume and elaborate toilet, and had placed herself at the table where Mandel and Benner sat. The latter always appeared glad to see her, and joked and chatted with her, while Mandel was evidently annoyed by her presence, and did not try very hard to conceal his feelings.

An almost inquisitorial examination of Benner elicited the fact that his friend had confided to him that the model tormented him with her attentions, and so thrust herself upon him that he was at a loss what to do about it. He had thought seriously of giving up the picture he was at work on, so that she might have no excuse for coming to his studio. The same examination drew out the confession that he was in love with La Rose Blanche himself, and had been for some time.

Now the most plausible theory of the three officers was apparently well enough

supported by the fact to warrant a most
careful investigation. This theory was
based chiefly on the common French axiom
that a woman is at the bottom of every
piece of mischief. The strongest suspicion
pointed towards La Rose Blanche, and no
motive but that of jealousy could be as-
signed for the deed. It was necessary,
then, to find some cause for jealousy before this theory could be accepted. Mandel was, as the study of his character had
proved to the officers, of a quiet and peace-
able disposition, and not in the habit of
frequenting society. Although, like most
young men, he spent part of his time in
the café, he was more disposed to stay at
home than to join in any time-killing amusement. After the most diligent search, the
officers only succeeded in finding one girl
besides La Rose Blanche who had been at
all on friendly terms with the artist. She
was a model who had posed for a picture he
painted while he occupied a studio in Rue
Monsieur le Prince, in the Latin Quarter.
But it was also found out that La Rose

Blanche had never seen Mandel until long after the picture was finished and the model dismissed. In this way the investigation went on with all possible ingenuity and most wearisome deliberation. No effort was more fruitful than the one just described. Every clue which promised to lead to the slightest knowledge of the life of the artist or the character of the model was followed out persistently, doggedly, and often even cruelly. Thus months passed.

Benner had been discharged from custody after his first long and trying examination. Unable to work, he wandered around the city in an aimless way. He could not help having a faint yet agonizing glimmer of hope that he might meet with a solution of the mystery of his friend's death. This solution would, he was sure, prove La Rose Blanche innocent. His unfinished statue in the clay, moistened only at irregular intervals, cracked and shrunk, and gradually fell to pieces. Dust settled in his studio, and his modelling tools rusted where they lay. At first he had tried to work, and, summoning another model, he had uncovered the clay. But he only spoiled what he touched, and after a short time he threw down his tools and walked away.

La Rose Blanche languished in the house of detention. Benner gradually began to lose courage, and perhaps even his faith wavered a little. When he learned that in the course of the examination the sleepy concierge of the house where the model lived had testified that she was absent all night at the time of the tragedy, Benner felt convinced that circumstances had combined to convict the girl. Her explanation had been most unsatisfactory. She had quarrelled with the artist because he told her he was annoyed by her. She did not remember what she said or did; she only knew that she left the house in a great passion, and walked the streets all night in the rain. Her passion gave way to her affection for the artist, and as soon as it was light she went to the studio to ask him to forgive her. She found him dead.

It was the apathy of La Rose Blanche

quite as much as her inability to prove herself innocent that caused the increasing un-
easiness in Benner's mind. Not that he believed her for a moment guilty, but he knew
that she was convicting herself with fatal
rapidity. He, knowing her character, could
understand how she could walk the streets
all night in the storm. He, in the warmth
of his passion for her, had often fought with
the weather for the relief the struggle afforded him. Love-madness is nothing new,
and the model's actions were only one phase
of it. At the little Café du Rat Mort, Benner now spent all his evenings, and on some
days part of the afternoon. He grew to be
one of the fixtures of the establishment.
The habitués of the place had ceased to talk
about him, and no longer pointed him out
to the new-comers as the friend of the dead
artist. The self-consciousness, which in the
beginning was painful to him, gradually wore
away, and he almost forgot himself at times
in connection with the tragedy, and only
kept constantly a dull sense of waiting—
waiting for he knew not what. Evening

after evening he sat at the little corner table
of the front room of the café, smoking cigar-
ettes, playing with the curious long-handled
spoons, and occasionally sipping coffee or a
glass of beer. The two tables between his
seat and the window on the street changed
occupants many times during the evening,
and the newspapers grew sticky, fumbled,
and worn at the hands of the frequent read-
ers. The opposite side of this room of the
café was filled by a long counter, covered on
top with shining zinc, and divided into several compartments, on the highest of which
stood the water carafes and a filter. Behind
this counter sat Madame Lépic, the wife of
the proprietor, placidly knitting from morning until midnight. When the street door
opened she raised her eyes and greeted the
comer with a hospitable smile ; then her face
resumed its normal expression of content-
ment. By carefully watching her it could be
discovered that she had a habit of quickly
glancing out from under her eyebrows and
taking in the whole interior of the café in a
flash of her dark little eye. Just beyond the

3

end of the counter a partition, wainscoted as high as a man's shoulder and with glass above, divided the café into two rooms. From where she sat Madame Lépic could overlook the four tables in the inner room as well as the three in the front. Her habit of constant watchfulness was cultivated, of course, by the necessity of keeping run of the two tired-looking waiters, who, like the rest of their class, had the weakness of being tempted by the abundance of money which passed through their hands. The police had already approached Madame Lépic, and she had given her testimony in regard to the actions of the model with the two young men. The police would not have been Parisian if they had not engaged madame to keep an eye on Benner. If he had not been too much occupied with his own thoughts, he might have detected her watching him constantly and persistently, even after he had ceased to be interesting in the eyes of the old habitués of the café.

It was a long four months after that terrible morning when Benner sat, late one after-

noon, in the café brooding as usual. Before
him on the stained marble slab stood a glass
of water, a tall goblet and long spoon with
twisted handle, and a porcelain match-holder
half full of matches. Bent over the table,
Benner was absent-mindedly arranging bits
of matches on the slab, something in the
shape of a guillotine. There were few people in the café. The click of the dominoes
in the back room, an occasional word from
one of the players, and the snap, snap, of
Madame Lépic's needles alone broke the
quiet of the interior. As Benner sat watching the outline of the guillotine he had
formed of broken matches, he saw one of the
corner pieces straighten out, and thus destroy
the symmetry of the arrangement. This was
a piece which had been bent at right angles
and only half broken off. Without paying
particular attention to the occurrence, he
took up the bit, threw it on the floor, and
put another one, similarly broken, in its
place. In a few moments this straightened
out also, and this time the movement attracted Benner's curiosity. Throwing it

aside, he replaced it by a fresh piece, and
this repeated the movement of the first two.
Now his curiosity was excited in earnest, and
his face and figure expressed such unusual
interest that the sharp glitter was visible under Madame Lépic's eyebrows, and her knitting went on only spasmodically. A fourth,
fifth, and sixth piece was put in place on the
corner of the little guillotine, and as the last
one was moving in the same way as the first
one did, Benner perceived that the water
spilled on the table trickled down to where
the broken match was placed. He took another match, as if to break it, but before the
brittle wood snapped, his face lit up with a
sudden expression of surprise and joy, and
he started to his feet so violently as to nearly throw the marble slab from the iron legs.
The click of the dominoes ceased, faces were
seen at the glass of the partition, and Madame
Lépic fairly stared, forgetting for once her
rôle of disinterested knitter.

Without stopping to pay, without seeming
to see anybody or anything, Benner strode
nervously and quickly out of the café. When

he was gone, Madame Lépic touched her bell,
one of the drowsy waiters came, received a
whispered order, and went out of the front
door hatless. A few moments later, even
before Benner had disappeared along the
boulevard in the direction of his studio, a
neatly dressed man came out of the police
station near the café and walked in the same
direction the sculptor had taken. After Benner had entered the *porte-cochère* of the great
building where his studio was, the police
agent went into the concierge's little office
near the door, and sat there as if he were at
home. In a few moments a nervous step
was heard on the asphalt of the court-yard,
and the agent had only time to withdraw
into the gloom of the corner behind the
stove when Benner passed out again, looking
neither to the right nor the left. He was
evidently much excited, and clutched rather
than held a small parcel in his hand. The
agent followed him a short distance behind,
and, meeting a *sergent de ville*, paused to say
a word to him. As Benner climbed on the
top of an Odéon omnibus, the agent took a

seat inside. Benner had not reached the interior boulevard before his studio was searched.

It was now nearly six o'clock, and the omnibus was crowded all the way across the city. As soon as the foot of the Rue des Beaux Arts was reached, Benner hurriedly descended, without waiting to stop the omnibus, and ran to the Academy. Here he sought the concierge, asked him a few questions, and then walked quickly away to the east side of the Luxembourg Gardens, where he rang the bell at the door of a house. He asked the servant who answered the bell if Professor Brunin was at home, and was evidently chagrined at being told he was absent and would not return for an hour or two. Entering the nearest café, he called for pen and paper, and wrote three pages rapidly, but legibly. By this time he had grown calmer in mind, not losing, however, the physical spring which his first excitement had induced. When his letter was finished he put it in an envelope, addressed it, and left it at the professor's house. This done, he walked rapidly across the Luxembourg Gardens to the Odéon, took an omnibus, accompanied as before by the agent, and at the end of the route, in the Place Pigalle, he descended, hastened to his studio, and did not come out again that evening. The great window was lighted all night long, and the agent in the entry could hear sawing, hammering, and filing at intervals, as he listened at the door every hour or two.

The gray morning broke, and Benner was still at his work. As the daylight dimmed the light of the lamp, he seemed not to notice it, but continued bent over his table, where various blocks, pieces of sheet brass, and a few tools were scattered promiscuously about. A piece of brown paper lay on the floor with what appeared to be a glove. On the corner of the table was a rude imitation of a human hand made of wood, hinged so that the fingers would move. This was not of recent construction ; but on a small drawing-board, over which Benner was leaning, was fixed a curious piece of mechanism which he was adjusting, having apparently just put it in

working order. He had joined together five
pieces of oak-wood, about three quarters of
an inch wide and half an inch thick, arranged
according to their length. The joints had
been cut in the shape of quarter - circles,
like the middle hinge of a carpenter's rule.
After these were fitted to each other, a saw-
cut was made in each one, and a piece of
sheet brass inserted which joined the concave
to the convex end. Two rivets on one end
and one on the other, serving as a pivot,
completed the hinge. The joints were so
arranged that, when opened to the greatest
extent, the five pieces composing the whole
made a straight line. The longest piece of
wood was fastened at the middle and outer
end by screws, which held it firmly to the
drawing-board. The shortest piece, on the
opposite end of the line, had attached to it
on the under side a pointed bit of brass like
an index. As morning broke, Benner was engaged in fixing a bit of an ivory metre meas-
ure, which is marked to millimetres, under-
neath this index point. After this scale was
securely fastened in its place the mechanism

was evidently completed, for he straightened
up, looked at his work from a distance, then
bent over it again, and gently tried the joints,
watching with some satisfaction the index as
it moved along the scale. While preoccupied with this study, a sudden knock at the
door caused him to start like a guilty man.
He threw open the door almost tragically.
It was only the concierge, who brought him
a letter. He tore it open, and read it and
re-read it with eagerness; then went to the
table and carefully measured several times
the whole length of the mechanism, from the
inner screw of the longest piece to the end
of the shortest. He then began to calculate
and to cipher on the edge of the drawing-
board. The letter read as follows:

"MONSIEUR,— En fait de renseignements sur la
dilatation du bois je ne connais que ceux donnés par
M. Reynaud dans son traité d'architecture, vol. i.,
pages 84 à 87 de la 2ᵉ êdition.

" Il en résulte que :

" 1. Les bois verts se dilatent beaucoup plus que
ceux purgés de sève.

" 2. Que le chêne se dilate tantôt plus tantôt moins
que le sapin, mais plus que le noyer.

" 3. Que dans les conditions ordinaires, c'est à dire, avec les variations hygrométriques de l'air seulement, le coefficient de dilatation atteint au plus 0.018, d'où résulte qu'une planche de 0.20 deviendrait 0.2036.

" 4. Qu'en plongeant dans l'eau pendant longtemps une planche primitivement très sèche, le coefficient de dilatation peut atteindre 0.0375, ce que donnerait pour la planche de 0.20, 0.2075.

" Peut-être vous trouverez d'autres renseignements dans le traité de charpente du Colonel Emy, ou dans celui de menuiserie de Roubo.

"Recevez, Monsieur, l'assurance de mes sentiments distingués.   P. BRUNIN."

A few days later there was gathered in a small room in the prefecture quite a knot of advocates and police officers. They were soon joined by Benner himself, accompanied by a short, stout gentleman with eye-glasses. Besides the ordinary furniture of the room, there was a wash-tub, a pail of water, a manikin, and the drawing-board with the mechanism on it. The entrance of the judge put a stop to the buzz of conversation, and when he took a seat on the low platform the rest of the company placed themselves on the benches in front. The judge, after a few preliminary remarks on the subject of the mystery of Montmartre, said that there had lately been developed such a new and surprising theory to account for the death of the artist that he had consented to give a hearing to the explanation of the theory. Benner then arose and made the following statement: " In the Café du Rat Mort, a few days ago, I noticed a peculiar movement in a broken match as it lay on the table before me. At first my curiosity was excited only to a moderate degree, but shortly this inexplicable motion interested me so that I experimented until I found the cause of it. At the same moment there flashed into my mind what I had learned long ago at school about capillary force, and the solution of the mystery of my friend's death was at once plain to me. Hurrying to my studio, I cut off the hand of my manikin, and carried it to the Academy of Fine Arts to show it to Professor Brunin, of the Architectural Department, and ask his assistance. Finding him neither there nor at his house, I wrote him a note and left it

for him. All that night I worked constructing a working model of a manikin's finger,
and the next morning I received a letter
from Professor Brunin which gave me the
data I was in search of—the facts in regard
to the expansion of wood when moistened.
I should read that letter here, but Professor
Brunin is present, and will explain the phenomenon. My theory is very simple. My
friend Charles Mandel was shot by his own
manikin. There are witnesses enough to
prove that the pistol had been loaded for a
long time, and that Mandel had often tried
in vain to draw the charge. It is also well
known that the pistol was cocked when it
was in the manikin's belt, for on the half-
completed picture it was so painted by Mandel on the last day of his life. Furthermore,
the position of the right index finger of the
manikin can also be plainly seen in the picture; for the artist, not having a model to
hold the weapon, had roughly rubbed in the
angular fingers of the lay figure, preparatory
to finishing the hand from life. The pistol
then, being loaded and cocked, needed but

the pressure of the finger to discharge it. That pressure was given by the rain on the night of the death of my friend. The lieutenant will find, on reference to his notebook, that on the morning when he examined the studio there had been quite a serious leak in the ceiling, and that the water had fallen directly on the manikin. He will find also in his notes the exact position of the manikin in reference to the divan on which the corpse lay. Now, it is clear that when the wrist of the manikin was bent, and the index finger was placed on the trigger of the pistol, only a very slight motion of the whole was necessary to give the pressure required to fire a pistol. The weapon was braced against the inside of the thumb of the hand, and thus held firmly there as it stuck in the belt ready to be drawn and fired. When the water first fell from the ceiling, it soaked the covering of the wrist and hand, and swelled the wrist joint so that it became absolutely immovable. Next the moisture extended to the tip of the fingers, the hand being held somewhat downward. In the manikin we have here, the exact construction of the fingers and the movement of the joints of the hand and wrist can be plainly seen. In my working model I have imitated the mechanism of one finger, so arranging it that the least deflection of the finger from the straight line will be measured on a scale of millimetres. The joints are so constructed that any elongation of the pieces of wood will curve the line of joints away from the straight line which I have drawn on the board. I propose to experiment with this model so as to make it perfectly plain that my friend's death was accidental. If the experiment were tried on the manikin, and with a flint-lock pistol, it would doubtless fail ninety-nine cases out of a hundred. In the accident which caused my friend's death everything happened to be perfectly adjusted. If my model works, of course the manikin might have worked in exactly the same way."

The lieutenant gave his explanation of the position in which the body was found, and added that he had calculated at the time that the shot must have been fired from the

direction of the manikin, and from about the
height of its waist. He found in his notes
the statement that the roof had leaked, and
the manikin was wet. Furthermore, the pistol was found just where the recoil would
have thrown it backward out of the manikin's hand. He ended by declaring that the
theory just advanced was new to him then,
and that he was convinced of its probability
by the manner in which it harmonized with
the conditions of the tragedy.

The professor proceeded next to give a full
account of the expansion of wood by moisture, and went into the study of the whole
phenomenon of capillary force. He was
somewhat verbose in his statement, probably because he, like other regular lecturers,
had been accustomed to spread a very little
fact over a great deal of time. His closing
argument in favor of the theory set forth by
Benner was this: " In the ancient quarries
wedges of wood were driven into holes in
the rock, water was poured on the wedges,
and the wood, expanding, split the solid
mass. Capillary force is irresistible. It was

this force which caused the deplorable accident which Mr. Benner has so ingeniously
and logically explained."

At the command of the judge the sculptor
proceeded with his experiment. He simply
fastened the drawing-board with the mechanism to the bottom of the inside of the tub by
means of screws. When it was in place it
was covered by about an inch of water. The
lieutenant then recorded on his note-book
the time of day and the position of the index, and every one present made mental
note of it. It was necessary, in order to give
the wood sufficient time to swell, to leave it
in the water for four or five hours. Consequently the judge adjourned the sitting until
the afternoon at four o'clock. The room was
locked and put in charge of the lieutenant
and two men.

When the same company assembled at the
appointed hour the door was opened by the
lieutenant, and the judge, with genuine human curiosity, stepped up to the tub, looked
into it, and gave an exclamation of surprise.
The others approached and looked in. The

lieutenant announced, almost triumphantly, that the index had moved seven millimetres —enough to have fired a cannon. The judge turned to the excited company and said, simply, "Messieurs, it was a capillary crime."

4

A FADED SCAPULAR

A FADED SCAPULAR

W E are seldom able to trace our individual superstitions to any definite
cause, nor can we often account for the peculiar sensations developed in us by the inexplicable and mysterious incidents in our
experience. Much of the timidity of childhood may be traced to early training in the
nursery, and sometimes the moral effects of
this weakness cannot be eradicated through
a lifetime of severe self-control and mental
suffering. The complicated disorders of the
imagination which arise from superstitious
fears can frequently be accounted for only
by inherited characteristics, by peculiar sen-
sitiveness to impressions, and by an overpow-
ering and perhaps abnormally active imagination. I am sure I am confessing to no
unusual characteristic when I say that I have

felt from childhood a certain sentiment or sensation in regard to material things which I can trace to no early experience, to the influence of no literature, and to no possible source, in fact, but that of inherited disposition.

The sentiment I refer to is this : whatever has belonged to or has been used by any person seems to me to have received some special quality, which, though often invisible and still oftener indefinable, still exists in a more or less strong degree, according to the amount of the impressionable power, if I may call it so, which distinguished the possessor. I am aware that this sentiment may be stigmatized as of the school-girl order ; that it is, indeed, of the same kind and class with that which leads an otherwise honest person to steal a rag from a famous battle flag, a leaf from an historical laurel wreath, or even to cut a signature or a title-page from a precious volume ; but with me the feeling has never taken this turn, else I should not have confessed to the possession of it. Whatever may be said or believed, however, I must refer to it in more or less comprehensible terms, because it may explain the conditions, although it will not unveil the causes, of the incidents I am about to describe with all honesty and frankness.

Nearly twenty years ago I made my first visit to Rome, long before it became the centre of the commercial and political activity of Italy, and while it was yet unspoiled for the antiquarian, the student, the artist, and the traveller. Never shall I forget the first few hours I spent wandering aimlessly through the streets—so far as I then knew, a total stranger in the city, with no distinct plan of remaining there, and with only the slight and imperfect knowledge of the place that one gains from the ordinary travellers' descriptions. The streets, the houses, the people, the strange sounds and stranger sights, the life so entirely different from what I had hitherto seen—all this interested me greatly. Far more powerful and far more vivid and lasting, however, was the impression of an inconceivable number of presences —I hesitate to call them spirits—not visible, of course, nor tangible, but still oppressing

me mentally and morally, exactly the same
as my physical self is often crushed and over-
powered in a great assembly of people. I
walked about, visited the cafés and concert-
halls, and tried in various ways to shake off
the uncomfortable feeling of ghostly company, but was unsuccessful, and went to my
lodgings much depressed and nervous. I
took my note-book, and wrote in it: " Rome
has been too much lived in. Among the
multitude of the dead there is no room for
the living." It seemed then a foolish mem-
orandum to write, and now, as I look at the
half-effaced pencil lines, I wonder why I was
not ashamed to write it. Yet there it is before me, a witness to my sensations at the
time, and the scrawl has even now the power
to bring up to me an unpleasantly vivid
memory of that first evening in Rome.

After a few days passed in visiting the galleries and the regular sights of the town, I
began to look for a studio and an apartment,
and finally found one in the upper story of a
house on the Via di Ripetta. Before moving
into the studio, I met an old friend and fel-

low-artist, and, as there was room enough for
two, gladly took him in with me.

The studio, with apartment, in the Via di
Ripetta was by no means unattractive.   It
was large, well lighted, comfortably and abun-
dantly furnished.   It was, as I have said, at
the top of the house; the studio overlooked
the Tiber, and the sitting-room and double-
bedded sleeping-room fronted the street. The
large studio window was placed rather high
up, so that the entrance door—a wide, heavy
affair, with large hinges and immense complicated lock and a " judas"—opened from
the obscurity of the hall directly under the
large window into the full light of the studio.
The roof of the house slanted from back to
front, so that the two rooms were lower
studded than the studio, and an empty space
or low attic opening into the studio above
them was partly concealed by an ample and
ragged curtain.   The fireplace was in the
middle of the left wall as you entered the
studio ; the door into the sitting-room was
in the farther right-hand corner, and the bedroom was entered by a door on the right-

hand wall of the sitting-room, so that the bedroom formed a wing of the studio and sitting-room, and from the former, looking through two doors, the bedroom window and part of the street wall could be seen. Both the beds were hidden from sight of any one in the studio, even when the doors were open.

The apartment was furnished in a way which denoted a certain amount of liberality, but everything was faded and worn, though not actually shabby or dirty. The carpets were threadbare, the damask-covered sofa and chairs showed marks of the springs, and the gimp was fringed and torn off in places. The beds were not mates; the basin and ewer were of different patterns; the few pictures on the wall were, like everything else in the place, curiously gray and dusty-looking, as if they had been shut up in the darkened rooms for a generation. Beyond the fireplace in the studio, the corner of the room was partitioned off by a dingy screen, six feet high or more, fixed to the floor for the space of two yards,

with one wing which shut like a door, enclosing a small space fitted up like a minia-
ture scullery, with a curious and elaborate
collection of pots and pans and kitchen uten-
sils, all hung in orderly rows, but every article with marks of service on it, and more
recent and obtrusive traces of long disuse.

In one of the first days of my search for a
studio I had found and inspected this very
place, but it had given me such a disagreeable feeling—it had seemed so worn out, so
full of relics of other people—that I could
not make up my mind to take it. After a
thorough search and diligent inquiry, however, I came to the conclusion that there
was absolutely no other place in Rome at
that busy season where I could set up my
easel, and, after having the place recommend-
ed to me by all the artists I called upon as a
well-known and useful studio, and a great
find at the busy season of the year, I took a
lease of the place for four months.

My friend and I moved in at the same
time, and I will not deny that I planned
to be supported by his presence at the mo-

ment of taking possession. When we arrived and had our traps all deposited in the middle of the studio, there came over the spirits of us both a strange gloom, which the bustle and confusion of settling did not in the least dispel. It was nearly dark that winter afternoon before we had finished unpacking, and the street lights were burning before we reached the little restaurant in the Via Quattro Fontane, where we proposed to take our meals. There was a cheerful company of artists and architects assembled there that evening, and we sat over our wine long after dinner. When the jolly party at last dispersed, it was well past midnight.

How gloomy the outer portal of the high building looked as we crossed the dimly lighted street and pushed open the back door! A musty, damp smell, like the atmosphere of the catacombs, met us as we entered. Our footsteps echoed loud and hollow in the empty corridor, and the large wax match I struck as we came in gave but a flickering light, which dimly shadowed the outline of the stone stairway, and threw the

rest of the corridor into a deep and mysterious gloom. We tramped up the five long
flights of stone stairs without a word, the
echo of our footsteps sounding louder and
louder, and the murky space behind us deep-
ening into the damp darkness of a cavern.
At last, after what seemed an interminable
climb, we came to the studio entrance. I
put the large key in the lock, turned it, and
pushed open the door. A strong draught,
like the lifeless breath from the mouth of a
tunnel, extinguished the match and left us
in darkness. I hesitated an instant, instinctively dreading to enter, and then went in,
followed by my friend, who closed the door
behind us. The heavy hinges creaked, the
door shut into the jambs with a solid thud,
the lock sprang into place with a sharp click,
and a noise like the clanging of a prison gate
resounded and re-echoed through the corridor and through the spacious studio. I felt
as if we were shut in from the whole world.

Lighting all the candles at hand and stir-
ring up the fire, we endeavored to make the
studio look cheerful, and, neither of us being

inclined to go to bed, we sat for a long time talking and smoking. But even the bright fire and the soothing tobacco smoke did not wholly dispel the gloom of the place, and when we finally carried the candles into the bedroom, I felt a vague sense of dismal anticipation and apprehension. We left both doors open, so that the light from our room streamed across the corner of the sitting-room, and threw a great square of strong reflection on the studio carpet. While undressing, I found that I had left my match-box on the studio table, and thought I would return for it. I remember now what a mental struggle I went through before I made up my mind to go without a candle. I glanced at my friend's face, partly to see if he noticed any indication of nervousness in my expression, and partly because I was conscious of a kind of psychological sympathy between us. But fear of his ridicule made me effectually conceal my feelings, and I went out of the room without speaking. As I walked across the non-resonant, carpeted stone floor I had the most curious set of sensations I have ever experienced. At nearly every step I took I came into a different stratum or perpendicular layer of air. First it was cool to my face, then warm, then chill again, and again warm. Thinking to calm my nervous excitement, I stood still and looked around me. The great window above my head dimly transmitted the sky reflection, but threw little light into the studio. The folds of the curtain over the open space above the sitting-room appeared to wave slightly in the uncertain light, and the easels and lay figure stood gaunt and ghostly along the further wall. I waited there and reasoned with myself, arguing that there was no possible cause for fear, that a strong man ought to control his nerves, that it was silly at my time of life to begin to be afraid of the dark; but I could not get rid of the sensation. As I went back to the bedroom I experienced the same succession of physical shocks; but whether they followed each other in the same order or not I was unable to determine.

It was some time before I could get to

sleep, and I opened my eyes once or twice before I lost consciousness. From the bedroom window there was a dim, very dim, light on the lace curtains, but the window itself was visible as a square mass, and did not appear to illuminate the room in the least. Suddenly, after a dreamless sleep of some duration, I awoke as completely as if I had been startled by a loud noise. The lace curtains were now quite brilliantly lighted from somewhere, I could not tell where, but the window itself seemed to be as little luminous as when I went to sleep. Without moving my head, I turned my eyes in the direction of the studio, and could see the open door as a dark patch in the gray wall, but nothing more. Then, as I was looking again at the curious illumination of the curtains, a moving mass came into the angle of my vision out of the corner of the room near the head of the bed, and passed slowly into full view between me and the curtain. It was unmistakably the figure of a man, not unlike that of the better type of Italian, and was dressed in the commonly worn soft hat and ample

cloak.   His profile came out clearly against
the light background of the lace curtain, and
showed him to be a man of considerable re-
finement of feature.   He did not make an
actually solid black silhouette against the
light, neither was the figure translucent, but
was rather like an object seen through a vapor or through a sheet of thin ground glass.

I tried to raise my head, but my nerve
force seemed suddenly to fail me, and while
I was wondering at my powerlessness, and
reasoning at the same time that it must be
a nightmare, the figure had moved slowly
across in front of the window, and out through
the open door into the studio.

I listened breathlessly, but not a sound did
I hear from the next room.   I pinched myself, opened and shut my eyes, and noticed
that the breathing of my room-mate was irregular, and unlike that of a sleeping man.
I am unable to understand why I did not sit
up or turn over or speak to my friend to find
out if he were awake.   I was fully conscious
that I ought to do this, but something, I
know not what, forced me to lie perfectly

motionless watching the window. I heard my room-mate breathing, opened and shut my eyes, and was certain, indeed, that I was really awake. As I reasoned on the phenomenon, and came naturally to the unwilling conclusion that my hallucination was probably premonitory of malaria, my nerves grew quiet, I began to think less intensely, and then I fell asleep.

The next morning I awoke with a feeling of disagreeable anticipation. I was loath to rise, even though the warm Italian sunlight was pouring into the room and gilding the dingy interior with brilliant reflections. In spite of this cheering glow of sunshine, the rooms still had the same dead and uninhabited appearance, and the presence of my friend, a vigorous and practical man, seemed to bring no recognizable vitality or human element to counteract the oppressiveness of the place. Every detail of my waking dream or hallucination of the night before was perfectly fresh in my mind, and the sense of apprehension was still strong upon me.

The distracting operations of settling the

studio, and the frequent excursions to neighboring shops to buy articles necessary to our
meagre housekeeping, did much towards taking my mind off the incident of the night;
but every time I entered the sitting-room or
the bedroom it all came up to me with a vividness that made my nerves quiver. We ex-
plored all the corners and cupboards of the
place. We even crawled up over the sitting-
room behind the dingy curtain, where a large
quantity of disused frames and old stretchers
were packed away. We familiarized ourselves,
in fact, with every nook and cranny of each
room; moved the furniture about in a different order; hung up draperies and sketches; and in many ways changed the character
of the interior. The faded, weary-looking
widow from whom I had hired the place, and
who took care of the rooms, carried away to
her own apartment many of the most obnox-
ious trifles which encumbered the small tables,
the étagère, and the wall spaces. She sighed
a great deal as we were making the rapid
changes to suit our own taste, but made no ob-
jection, and we naturally thought it was the

regular custom of every new occupant to turn the place upside down.

Late in the afternoon I was alone in the studio for an hour or more, and sat by the fire trying to read. The daylight was not gone, and the rumble of the busy street came plainly to my ears. I say "trying to read," for I found reading quite impossible. The moment I began to fix my attention on the page, I had a very powerful feeling that some one was looking over my shoulder. Do what I would, I could not conquer the unreasonable sensation. Finally, after starting up and looking about me a dozen times, I threw down the book and went out. When I returned, after an hour in the open air, I found my friend walking up and down in the studio with open doors, and two guttering candles alight.

"It's a curious thing," he said, "I can't read this book. I have been trying to put my mind on it a whole half-hour, and I can't do it. I always thought I could get interested in 'Gaboriau' in a moment under any circumstances."

"I went out to walk because I couldn't manage to read," I replied, and the conversation ended.

We went to the theatre that evening, and afterwards to the Café Greco, where we talked art in half a dozen languages until midnight, and then came home. Our entrance to the house and the studio was much the same as on the previous night, and we went to bed without a word. My mind naturally reverted to the experience of the night before, and I lay there for a long time with my eyes open, making a strong effort of the imagination to account for the vision by the dim shapes of the furniture, the lace curtains, and the suggestive and shadowy perspective. But, although the interior was weird enough, by reason of the dingy hangings and the diffused light, I was unable to trace the origin of the illusion to any object within the range of my vision, or to account for the strange illumination which had startled me. I went to sleep thinking of other things, and with my nerves comparatively quiet.

Some time in the early morning, about three

o'clock, as near as I could judge, I slowly awoke, and saw the lace curtains illuminated as before. I found myself in an expectant frame of mind, neither calm nor excited, but rather in that condition of philosophical quiet which best prepared me for an investigation of the phenomenon which I confidently expected to witness. Perhaps this is assuming too eagerly the position of a philosopher, but I am certain no element of fear disturbed my reason, that I was neither startled nor surprised at awakening as I did, and that my mind was active and undoubtedly prepared for the investigation of the mystery.

I was therefore not at all shocked to observe the same shape come first into the angle of my eye, and then into the full range of my vision, next appear as a silhouette against the curtains, and finally lose itself in the darkness of the doorway. During the progress of the shape across the room I noticed the size and general aspect of it with keen attention to detail, and with satisfactory calmness of observation. It was only after the figure had passed out of sight, and the light on the window curtains grew dim again, much as an electric light loses its brilliancy with the diminution of the strength of the current, that it occurred to me to consider the fact that during the period of the hallucination I had been utterly motionless. There was not the slightest doubt of my being awake. My friend in the adjoining bed was breathing regularly, the ticking of my watch was plainly audible, and I could feel my heart beating with unusual rapidity and vigor.

The strange part of the whole incident was this incapacity of action; and the more I reasoned about it the more I was mystified by the utter failure of nerve force. Indeed, while the mind was actively at work on this problem, the physical torpor continued, a languor not unlike the incipient drowsiness of anæsthesia came gradually over me, and, though mentally protesting against the helpless condition of the body, and struggling to keep awake, I fell asleep, and did not stir till morning.

With the bright, clear winter's day returned the doubts and disappointments of the day before—doubts of the existence of the phenomenon, disappointment at the failure of any solution of the hallucination. A second day in the studio did little towards dispelling the mental gloom which possessed us both, and at night my friend confessed that he thought we must have stumbled into a malarial quarter.

At this distance of time it is absolutely incomprehensible to me how I could have gone on as I did from day to day, or rather from night to night—for the same hallucination was repeated nightly—without speaking to my friend, or at least taking some energetic steps towards an investigation of the mystery. But I had the same experience every night for fully a week before I really began to plan serious means of discovering whether it was an hallucination, a nightmare, or a flesh-and-blood intruder. First, I had some curiosity each night to see whether there would be a repetition of the incident. Second, I was eager to note any physical or mental symptom which would serve as a clue to the mystery. Pride, or some other equally authoritative sentiment, continued to keep me from disclosing my secret to my friend, although I was on the point of doing so on several occasions. My first plan was to keep a candle burning all night, but I could invent no plausible excuse to my comrade for this action. Next I proposed to shut the bedroom door, and on speaking of it to my friend, he strongly objected on the ground of the lack of ventilation, and was not willing to risk having the window open on account of the malaria. After all, since this was an entirely personal matter, it seemed to me the only thing to do was to depend on my own strength of mind and moral courage to solve this mystery unaided. I put my loaded revolver on the table by the bedside, drew back the lace curtain before going to bed, and left the door only half open, so I could not see into the studio. The night I made these preparations I awoke as usual, saw the same figure, but, as before, could not move a hand. After it had passed the window, I tried hard to bring myself to take my revolver, and find out whether I had to deal with a man or a simulacrum. But even while I was arguing with myself, and trying to find out why I could not move, sleep came upon me before I had carried out my purposed action.

The shock of the first appearance of the vision had been nearly overbalanced by my eagerness to investigate, and my intense interest in the novel condition of mind or body which made such an experience possible. But after the utter failure of all my schemes and the collapse of my theories as to evident causes of the phenomenon, I began to be harassed and worried, almost unconsciously at first, by the ever-present thought, the daily anticipation, and the increasing dread of the hallucination. The self-confidence that first supported me in my nightly encounter diminished on each occasion, and the curiosity which stimulated me to the study of the phenomenon rapidly gave way to the sentiment akin to terror, when I proved myself incapable of grappling with the mystery.

The natural result of this preoccupation was inability to work and little interest in

recreation, and as the long weeks wore away
I grew morose, morbid, and hypochondria-
cal. The pride which kept me from sharing
my secret with my friend also held me at
my post, and nerved me to endure the tor-
ment in the rapidly diminishing hope of
finally exorcising the spectre or recovering
my usual healthy tone of mind. The difficulty of my position was increased by the
fact that the apparition failed to appear occasionally; and while I welcomed each failure as a sign that the visits were to cease,
they continued spasmodically for weeks, and
I was still as far away from the interpreta-
tion of the problem as ever. Once I sought
medical advice, but the doctor could discover nothing wrong with me except what
might be caused by tobacco, and, following
his advice, I left off smoking. He said I
had no malaria; that I needed more exercise, perhaps; but he could not account for
my insomnia, for I, like most patients, had
concealed the vital facts in my case, and had
complained of insomnia as the cause of my
anxiety about my health.

The approach of spring tempted me out of doors, and in the warm villa gardens and the sun-bathed Campagna I could sometimes forget the nightmare that haunted me. This was not often possible, unless I was in the company of cheerful companions, and I grew to dread the hour when I was to return to the studio after an excursion into the country among the soothing signs of returning summer. To shut the clanging door of the studio was to place an impenetrable barrier between me and the outside world; and the loneliness of that interior seemed to be only intensified by the presence of my companion, who was apparently as much depressed in spirits as myself.

We made various attempts at the entertainment of friends, but they all lacked that element of spontaneous fun which makes such occasions successful, and we soon gave it up. On pleasant days we threw open the windows on the street to let in the warm air and sunshine, but this did not seem to drive away the musty odors of the interior. We were much too high up to feel any neighborly proximity to the people on the other side of the street. The chimney-pots and irregular roofs below and beyond were not very cheerful objects in the view; and the landlady, who, as far as we knew, was the only other occupant of the upper story, did not give us a great sense of companionship. Never once did I enter the studio without feeling the same curious sensation of alternate warm and cool strata of air. Never for a quarter of an hour did I succeed in reading a book or a newspaper, however interesting it might be. We frequently had two models at a time, and both my friend and myself made several beginnings of pictures, but neither of us carried the work very far.

On one occasion a significant remark was made by a lady friend who came to call. She will undoubtedly remember now when she reads these lines that she said, on leaving the studio : " This is a curiously draughty place. I feel as if it had been blowing hot and cold on me all the time I have been here, and yet you have no windows open."

At another time my comrade burst out as I was going away one evening about eleven o'clock to a reception at one of the palaces : " I wish you wouldn't go in for society so much.   I can't go to the café ; all the fellows go home about this time of the evening.   I don't like to stay here in this dismal hole, all cooped up by myself.   I can't read, I can't sleep, and I can't think."

It occurred to me that it was a little queer for him to object to being left alone, unless he, like myself, had some disagreeable experiences there, and I remembered that he had usually gone out when I had, and was seldom, if ever, alone in the studio when I returned.   His tone was so peevish and impatient that I thought discussion was injudicious, and simply replied, " Oh, you're bilious ; I'll be home early," and went away.   I have often thought since that it was the one occasion when I could have easily broached the subject of my mental trouble, and I have always regretted I did not do so.

Matters were brought to a climax in this way : My friend was summoned to America

by telegraph a little more than two months
after we took the studio, and left me at a
day's notice. The amount and kind of moral
courage I had to summon up before I could
go home alone the first evening after my
comrade left me can only be appreciated by
those who have undergone some similar tort-
ure. It was not like the bracing up a man
goes through when he has to face some imminent known danger, but was of a more
subtle and complex kind. "There is nothing to fear," I kept saying to myself, and
yet I could not shake off a nameless dread.
"You are in your right mind and have all
your senses," I continually argued, "for you
see and hear and reason clearly enough. It
is a brief hallucination, and you can conquer
the mental weakness which causes it by per-
sistent strength of will. If it be a simulacrum, you, as a practical man, with good
physical health and sound enough reasoning
powers, ought to investigate it to the best
of your ability." In this way I endeavored
to nerve myself up, and went home late, as
usual. The regular incident of the night

occurred. I felt keenly the loss of my friend's companionship, and suffered accordingly, but in the morning I was no nearer to the solution of the mystery than I was before.

For five weary, torturing nights did I go up to that room alone, and, with no sound of human proximity to cheer me or to break the wretched feeling of utter solitude, I endured the same experience. At last I could bear it no longer, and determined to have a change of air and surroundings. I hastily packed a travelling-bag and my color-box, leaving all my extra clothes in the wardrobes and the bureau drawers, told the landlady I should return in a week or two, and paid her for the remainder of the time in advance. The last thing I did was to take my travelling-cap, which hung near the head of my bead. A break in the wall-paper showed that there was a small door here. Pulling the knob which had held my cap, the door was readily opened, and disclosed a small niche in the wall. Leaning against the back of the niche was a small crucifix with a rude figure of Christ, and suspended from the neck of the image by a small cord was a triangular object covered with faded cloth. While I was examining with some interest the hiding-place of these relics, the landlady entered.

" What are these?" I asked.

" Oh, signore!" she said, half sobbing as she spoke. " These are relics of my poor husband. He was an artist like yourself, signore. He was—he was—ill, very ill—and in mind as well as body, signore. May the Blessed Virgin rest his soul! He hated the crucifix, he hated the scapular, he hated the priests. Signore, he—he died without the sacrament, and cursed the holy water. I have never dared to touch those relics, signore. But he was a good man, and the best of husbands;" and she buried her face in her hands.

I took the first train for Naples, and have never been in Rome since.

*   *   *   *   *

Three years later I was making an afternoon call in Boston, and met for the first

6

time since we parted in Rome the friend who had occupied the studio with me there.

When our greetings were over I asked, without any preliminary remark or explanation:

" Did you ever notice anything peculiar about that studio in Rome?"

" If you hadn't asked me that question," he replied, " I should have put a similar one to you. I remember it as the most dismal and oppressive place I ever was in. I had a constant presentiment that something terrible was going to happen there. The air in the studio was often cold and warm in streaks. I couldn't read, write, or paint without feeling that some one was looking over my shoulder. Every night I waked up towards morning and lay awake for some time, and often thought of speaking to find out whether you were awake too; for it seemed as if you must be, from your breathing. I couldn't bear to stay alone there either in the daytime or at night, and even now I would rather live in the catacombs than set my easel up in that studio again. Now, what made you ask me about it?"

" Because I have never felt quite certain that I was in my right mind during the season we spent in Rome, and the memory of that studio has always haunted me like a horrid dream," I replied. " Did you never have any hallucinations or nightmares there?"

" No," he said, " unless you call the whole thing a nightmare."

" Why didn't you say something to me about it at the time?" I asked.

" Why didn't you say something, if you felt as you say you did?" was his reply.

YATIL

YATIL

WHILE in Paris, in the spring of 1878, I witnessed an accident in a circus, which for a time made me renounce all athletic exhibitions. Six horses were stationed side by side in the ring before a spring-board, and the whole company of gymnasts ran and turned somersaults over the horses, alighting on a mattress spread on the ground. The agility of one finely developed young fellow excited great applause every time he made the leap. He would shoot forward in the air like a javelin, and in his flight curl up and turn over directly above the mattress, dropping on his feet as lightly as a bird. This play went on for some minutes, and at each round of applause the favorite seemed to execute his leap with increased skill and grace. Finally,

he was seen to gather himself a little farther
in the background than usual, evidently to
prepare for a better start. The instant his
turn came, he shot out of the crowd of attendants and launched himself into the
air with tremendous momentum. Almost
quicker than the eye could follow him, he
had turned and was dropping to the ground,
his arms held above his head, which hung
slightly forward, and his legs stretched to
meet the shock of the elastic mattress.

But this time he had jumped an inch too
far. His feet struck just on the edge of the
mattress, and he was thrown violently forward, doubling up on the ground with a
dull thump, which was heard all over the
immense auditorium. He remained a second or two motionless, then sprang to his
feet, and as quickly sank to the ground
again. The ring attendants and two or
three gymnasts rushed to him and took
him up. The clown, in evening dress, per-
sonating the mock ring-master, the conventional spotted merryman, and a stalwart
gymnast in buff fleshings, bore the drooping

form of the favorite in their arms, and, followed by the by-standers, who offered in-
effectual assistance, carried the wounded
man across the ring and through the draped
arch under the music gallery. Under any
other circumstances the group would have
excited a laugh, for the audience was in that
condition of almost hysterical excitement
when only the least effort of a clown is necessary to cause a wave of laughter. But the
moment the wounded man was lifted from
the ground, the whole strong light from the
brilliant chandelier struck full on his right
leg dangling from the knee, with the foot
hanging limp and turned inward. A deep
murmur of sympathy swelled and rolled
around the crowded amphitheatre.

I left the circus, and hundreds of others
did the same. A dozen of us called at the
box-office to ask about the victim of the
accident. He was advertised as " The
Great Polish Champion Bare-back Rider
and Aerial Gymnast." We found that he
was really a native of the East, whether
Pole or Russian the ticket-seller did not

know. His real name was Nagy, and he
had been engaged only recently, having returned a few months before from a profes-
sional tour in North America. He was supposed to have money, for he commanded a
good salary, and was sober and faithful.
The accident, it was said, would probably
disable him for a few weeks only, and then
he would resume his engagement.

The next day an account of the accident
was in the newspapers, and twenty-four
hours later all Paris had forgotten about it.
For some reason or other I frequently
thought of the injured man, and had an occasional impulse to go and inquire after
him; but I never went. It seemed to me
that I had seen his face before, when or
where I tried in vain to recall. It was not
an impressive face, but I could call it up at
any moment as distinct to my mind's eye as
a photograph to my physical vision. Whenever I thought of him, a dim, very dim
memory would flit through my mind, which
I could never seize and fix.

Two months later, I was walking up the Rue Richelieu, when some one, close beside me and a little behind, asked me in Hungarian if I was a Magyar. I turned quickly to answer no, surprised at being thus addressed, and beheld the disabled circus-rider. The feeling that I had met him before came upon me even stronger than at the time of the accident, and my puzzled expression was evidently construed by him into vexation at being spoken to by a stranger. He began to apologize for stopping me, and was moving away, when I asked him about the accident, remarking that I was present on the evening of his misfortune. My next question, put in order to detain him, was:

"Why did you ask if I was a Hungarian?"

"Because you wear a Hungarian hat," was the reply.

This was true. I happened to have on a little, round, soft felt hat, which I had purchased in Buda-Pesth.

"Well, but what if I were Hungarian?"

"Nothing; only I was lonely and wanted company, and you looked as if I had seen you somewhere before. You are an artist, are you not?"

I said I was, and asked him how he guessed it.

"I can't explain how it is," he said, "but I always knew them. Are you doing anything?"

"No," I replied.

"Perhaps I may get you something to do," he suggested. "What is your line?"

"Figures," I answered, unable to divine how he thought he could assist me.

This reply seemed to puzzle him a little, and he continued:

"Do you ride or do the trapeze?"

It was my turn now to look dazed, and it might easily have been gathered, from my expression, that I was not flattered at being taken for a sawdust artist. However, as he apparently did not notice any change in my face, I explained without further remark that I was a painter. The explanation did not seem to disturb him any: he was evidently acquainted with the profession, and looked upon it as kindred to his own.

As we walked along through the great open quadrangle of the Tuileries, I had an opportunity of studying his general appearance. He was neatly dressed, and, though pale, was apparently in good health. Notwithstanding a painful limp, his carriage was erect and his movements denoted great physical strength. On the bridge over the Seine we paused for a moment and leaned on the parapet, and thus, for the first time, stood nearly face to face. He looked earnestly at me a moment without speaking, and then, shouting "*Torino*" so loudly and earnestly as to attract the gaze of all the passers, he seized me by the hand, and continued to shake it and repeat "*Torino*" over and over again.

This word cleared up my befogged memory like magic. There was no longer any mystery about the man before me. The impulse which now drew us together was only the unconscious souvenir of an early acquaintance, for we had met before. With

the vision of the Italian city, which came
distinctly to my eyes at that moment, came
also to my mind every detail of an incident
which had long since passed entirely from
my thoughts.

It was during the Turin carnival in 1875
that I happened to stop over for a day and
a night, on my way down from Paris to
Venice.   The festival was uncommonly
dreary, for the air was chilly, the sky gray
and gloomy, and there was a total lack of
spontaneity in the popular spirit.   The
gaudy decorations of the Piazza and the
Corso, the numberless shows and booths,
and the brilliant costumes, could not make
it appear a season of jollity and mirth, for
the note of discord in the hearts of the
people was much too strong.   King Carnival's might was on the wane, and neither
the influence of the Church nor the encouragement of the State was able to bolster up
the superannuated monarch.   There was no
communicativeness in even what little fun
there was going, and the day was a long and

a tedious one. As I was strolling around
in rather a melancholy mood, just at the
close of the cavalcade, I saw the flaming
posters of a circus, and knew my day was
saved, for I had a great fondness for the
ring. An hour later I was seated in the
cheerfully lighted amphitheatre, and the old
performance of the trained stallions was going on as I had seen it a hundred times before. At last, the "Celebrated Cypriot
Brothers, the Universal Bare-back Riders,"
came tripping gracefully into the ring,
sprang lightly upon two black horses, and
were off around the narrow circle like the
wind, now together, now apart, performing
all the while marvellous feats of strength
and skill. It required no study to discover
that there was no relationship between the
two performers. One of them was a heavy,
gross, dark-skinned man, with the careless
bearing of one who had been nursed in
a circus. The other was a small, fair-haired
youth of nineteen or twenty years, with
limbs as straight and as shapely as the
Narcissus, and with joints like the wiry-

limbed fauns. His head was round, and his
face of a type which would never be called
beautiful, although it was strong in feature
and attractive in expression. His eyes were
small and twinkling, his eyebrows heavy,
and his mouth had a peculiar proud curl in
it which was never disturbed by the tame
smile of the practised performer. He was
evidently a foreigner. He went through his
acts with wonderful readiness and with slight
effort, and, while apparently enjoying keenly
the exhilaration of applause, he showed no
trace of the *blasé* bearing of the old stager.
In nearly every act that followed he took
a prominent part. On the trapeze, somer-
saulting over horses placed side by side,
grouping with his so-called brother and a small
lad, he did his full share of the work, and,
when the programme was ended, he came
among the audience to sell photographs
while the lottery was being drawn.

As usual during the carnival, there was a
lottery arranged by the manager of the
circus, and every ticket had a number which
entitled the holder to a chance in the prizes.

When the young gymnast came in turn to me, radiant in his salmon fleshings and blue trunks, with slippers and bows to match, I could not help asking him if he was an Italian.

"No, signore, Magyar!" he replied, and I shortly found that his knowledge of Italian was limited to a dozen words. I occupied him by selecting some photographs, and, much to his surprise, spoke to him in his native tongue. When he learned I had been in Hungary, he was greatly pleased, and the impatience of other customers for the photographs was the only thing that prevented him from becoming communicative immediately. As he left me I slipped into his hand my lottery-ticket, with the remark that I never had any luck, and hoped he would.

The numbers were, meanwhile, rapidly drawn, the prizes being arranged in the order of their value, each ticket taken from the hat denoting a prize, until all were distributed. "Number twenty-eight — a pair of elegant vases!" "Number sixteen—three bottles of vermouth!" "Number one hun-

7

dred and eighty-four—candlesticks and two bottles of vermouth!" "Number four hundred and ten—three bottles of vermouth and a set of jewelry!" "Number three hundred and nineteen—five bottles of vermouth!" and so on, with more bottles of vermouth than anything else. Indeed, each prize had to be floated on a few litres of the Turin specialty, and I began to think that perhaps it would have been better, after all, not to have given my circus friend the ticket if he were to draw drink with it.

Many prizes were called out, and at last only two numbers remained. The excitement was now intense, and it did not diminish when the conductor of the lottery announced that the last two numbers would draw the two great prizes of the evening, namely: An order on a Turin tailor for a suit of clothes, and an order on a jeweller for a gold watch and chain. The first of these two final numbers was taken out of the hat.

"Number twenty-five—order for a suit of clothes!" was the announcement.

Twenty-five had been the number of my

ticket. I did not hear the last number
drawn, for the Hungarian was in front of
my seat trying to press the order on me,
and protesting against appropriating my
good-luck. I wrote my name on the programme for him, with the simple address,
U. S. A., persuaded him to accept the wind-
fall, and went home. The next morning I
left town.

On the occasion of our mutual recognition in Paris, the circus-rider began to relate,
as soon as the first flush of his surprise was
over, the story of his life since the incident
in Turin. He had been to New York and
Boston, and all the large sea-coast towns;
to Chicago, St. Louis, and even to San
Francisco; always with a circus company.
Whenever he had had an opportunity in
the United States, he had asked for news
of me.

"The United States is so large!" he said,
with a sigh. "Every one told me that, when
I showed the Turin programme with your
name on it."

The reason why he had kept the pro-

gramme and tried to find me in America
was because the lottery-ticket had been the
direct means of his emigration, and, in fact,
the first piece of good-fortune that had be-
fallen him since he left his native town.
When he joined the circus he was an apprentice, and, besides a certain number of
hours of gymnastic practice daily and service in the ring both afternoon and evening,
he had half a dozen horses to care for, his
part of the tent to pack up and load, and
the team to drive to the next stopping-
place. For sixteen, and often eighteen hours
of hard work, he received only his food and
his performing clothes. When he was counted as one of the troupe his duties were
lightened, but he got only enough money to
pay his way with difficulty. Without a *lira*
ahead, and, with no clothes but his rough
working suit and his performing. costume,
he could not hope to escape from this sort
of bondage. The luck of number twenty-
five had put him on his feet.

"All Hungarians worship America," he
said, "and when I saw that you were an

American, I knew that my good-fortune had
begun in earnest. Of course, I believed
America to be the land of plenty, and there
could have been no stronger proof of this
than the generosity with which you, the first
American I had ever seen, gave me, a perfect stranger, such a valuable prize. When
I remembered the number of the ticket and
the letter in the alphabet, Y, to which this
number corresponds, I was dazed at the significance of the omen, and resolved at once
to seek my fortune in the United States.
I sold the order on the tailor for money
enough to buy a suit of ready-made clothes
and pay my fare to Genoa. From this
port I worked my passage to Gibraltar, and
thence, after performing a few weeks in a
small English circus, I went to New York
in a fruit-vessel. As long as I was in America everything prospered with me. I made
a great deal of money, and spent a great
deal. After a couple of years I went to
London with a company, and there lost my
pay and my position by the failure of the
manager. In England my good-luck all

left me. Circus people are too plenty there;
everybody is an artist. I could scarcely get
anything to do in my line, so I drifted over
to Paris."

We prolonged our stroll for an hour, for,
although I did not anticipate any pleasure
or profit from continuing the acquaintance,
there was yet a certain attraction in his simplicity of manner and in his naïve faith in
the value of my influence on his fortunes.
Before we parted he expressed again his
ability to get me something to do, but I did
not credit his statement enough to correct
the impression that I was in need of employment. At his earnest solicitation I gave
him my address, concealing, as well as I
could, my reluctance to encourage an acquaintance which would doubtless prove a
burden to me.

One day passed, and two, and, on the
third morning, the porter showed him to
my room.

"I have found you work!" he cried, in
the first breath.

Sure enough, he had been to a Polish

acquaintance who knew a countryman, a copyist in the Louvre. This copyist had a superabundance of orders, and was glad to get some one to help him finish them in haste. My gymnast was so much elated over his success at finding occupation for me that I hadn't the heart to tell him that I was at leisure only while hunting a studio. I therefore promised to go with him to the Louvre some day, but I always found an excuse for not going.

For two or three weeks we met at intervals. At various times, thinking he was in want, I pressed him to accept the loan of a few francs; but he always stoutly refused. We went together to his lodging-house, where the landlady, an Englishwoman, who boarded most of the circus people, spoke of her "poor, dear Mr. Nodge," as she called him, in quite a maternal way, and assured me that he had wanted for nothing, and should not as long as his wound disabled him. In the course of a few days I had gathered from him a complete history of his circus-life, which was full of adventure and hardship. When we met in Turin, he was, as I thought at the time, somewhat of a novice in the circus business, having left his home less than two years before. He had, indeed, been associated as a regular member of the company only a few months, after having served a difficult and wearing apprenticeship. He was born in Koloszvar, where his father was a professor in the university, and there he grew up with three brothers and a sister, in a comfortable home. He always had had a great desire to travel, and, from early childhood, developed a special fondness for gymnastic feats. The thought of a circus made him fairly wild. On rare occasions a travelling show visited this Transylvanian town, and his parents with difficulty restrained him from following the circus away. At last, in 1873, one show, more complete and more brilliant than any one before seen there, came on the newly opened railway, and he, now a man grown, went away with it, unable longer to restrain his passion for the profession. Always accustomed to horses, and already

a skilful acrobat, he was immediately accepted by the manager as an apprentice, and,
after a season in Roumania and a disastrous
trip through Southern Austria, they came
into Northern Italy, where I met him.

Whenever he spoke of his early life he always became quiet and depressed, and, for
a long time, I believed that he brooded over
his mistake in exchanging a happy home
for the vicissitudes of Bohemia. It came
out slowly, however, that he was haunted
by a superstition, a strange and ingenious
one, which was yet not without a certain
show of reason for its existence. Little by
little I learned the following facts about it:
His father was of pure Szeklar, or original
Hungarian, stock, as dark-skinned as a Hin-
doo, and his mother was from one of the
families of Western Hungary, with probably
some Saxon blood in her veins. His three
brothers were dark like his father, but he and
his sister were blondes. He was born with
a peculiar red mark on his right shoulder,
directly over the scapula. This mark was
shaped like a forked stick. His father had

received a wound in the insurrection of '48,
a few months before the birth of him, the
youngest son, and this birth-mark repro-
duced the shape of the father's scar. Among
Hungarians his father passed for a very
learned man. He spoke fluently German,
French, and Latin (the language used by
Hungarians in common communication with
other nationalities), and took great pains to
give his children an acquaintance with each
of these tongues. Their earliest playthings
were French alphabet-blocks, and the set
which served as toys and tasks for each of
the elder brothers came at last to him as his
legacy. The letters were formed by the human figure in different attitudes, and each
block had a little couplet below the picture,
beginning with the letter on the block. The
Y represented a gymnast hanging by his
hands to a trapeze, and, being a letter which
does not occur in the Hungarian language
except in combinations, excited most the
interest and imagination of the youngsters.
Thousands of times did they practise the
grouping of the figures on the blocks, and

the Y always served as a model for trapeze
exercises. My friend, on account of his
birth-mark, which resembled a rude Y, was
early dubbed by his brothers with the nick-
name Yatil, this being the first words of the
French couplet printed below the picture.
Learning the French by heart, they believed
the *Y a-t-il* to be one word, and, with boyish
fondness for nicknames, saddled the youngest with this. It is easy to understand how
the shape of this letter, borne on his body
in an indelible mark, and brought to his
mind every moment of the day, came to
seem in some way connected with his life.
As he grew up in this belief he became more
and more superstitious about the letter and
about everything in the remotest way connected with it.

The first great event of his life was join-
ing the circus, and to this the letter Y more
or less directly led him. He left home on
his twenty-fifth birthday, and twenty-five was
the number of the letter Y in the block-
alphabet.

The second great event of his life was the

Turin lottery, and the number of the lucky
ticket was twenty-five. "The last sign given
me," he said, "was the accident in the circus
here." As he spoke, he rolled up the right
leg of his trousers, and there, on the outside of the calf, about midway between the
knee and ankle, was a red scar forked like
the letter Y.

From the time he confided his superstition to me he sought me more than ever.
I must confess to feeling, at each visit of
his, a little constrained and unnatural. He
seemed to lean on me as a protector, and to
be hungry all the time for an intimate sympathy I could never give him. Although I
shared his secret, I could not lighten the
burden of his superstition. His wound had
entirely healed, but, as his leg was still weak
and he still continued to limp a little, he
could not resume his place in the circus.
Between brooding over his superstition and
worrying about his accident, he grew very
despondent. The climax of his hopelessness was reached when the doctor told him
at last that he would never be able to vault

again. The fracture had been a severe one,
the bone having protruded through the skin.
The broken parts had knitted with great
difficulty, and the leg would never be as
firm and as elastic as before. Besides, the
fracture had slightly shortened the lower
leg. His circus career was therefore ended,
and he attributed his misfortune to the ill-
omened letter Y.

Just about the time of his greatest despondency, war was declared between Russia and Turkey. The Turkish embassadors
were drumming up recruits all over Western Europe. News came to the circus board-
ing-house that good riders were wanted for
the Turkish mounted gendarmes. Nagy
resolved to enlist, and we went together to
the Turkish embassy. He was enrolled after
only a superficial examination, and was directed to present himself on the following
day to embark for Constantinople. He
begged me to go with him to the rendez-
vous, and there I bade him adieu. As I
was shaking his hand he showed me the
certificate given him by the Turkish embas-

sador. It bore the date of May 25, and at
the bottom was a signature in Turkish characters which could be readily distorted by
the imagination into a rude and scrawling Y.

A series of events occurring immediately
after Nagy left for Constantinople resulted
in my own unexpected departure for the
seat of war in a civil capacity in the Russian
army. The series of curious coincidences
in the experience of the circus-rider had impressed me very much when he related them,
but in the excitement of the Turkish campaign I entirely forgot him and his story. I
do not, indeed, recall any thought of Nagy
during the first five months in the field. The
day after the fall of Plevna I rode towards the
town through the line of deserted earthworks.
The dead were lying where they had fallen in
the dramatic and useless sortie of the day
before. The corpses on a battle-field always
excite fresh interest, no matter if the spectacle be an every-day one; and as I rode
slowly along I studied the attitudes of the
dead soldiers, speculating on the relation be-

tween the death-poses and the last impulse
that had animated the living frame. Behind
a rude barricade of wagons and household
goods, part of the train of non-combatants
which Osman Pasha had ordered to accompany the army in the sortie, a great number
of dead lay in confusion. The peculiar position of one of these instantly attracted my
eye. He had fallen on his face against the
barricade, with both arms stretched above
his head, evidently killed instantly. The figure on the alphabet-block, described by the
circus-rider, came immediately to my mind.
My heart beat as I dismounted and looked
at the dead man's face. It was unmistakably
Turkish.

This incident revived my interest in the
life of the circus-rider, and gave me an impulse to look among the prisoners to see if
by chance he might be with them. I spent
a couple of days in distributing tobacco and
bread in the hospitals and among the thirty
thousand wretches herded shelterless in the
snow. There were some of the mounted
gendarmes among them, and I even found

several Hungarians; but none of them had
ever heard of the circus-rider.

The passage of the Balkans was a campaign full of excitement, and was accompanied by so much hardship that selfishness
entirely got the upperhand of me, and life
became a battle for physical comfort. After
the passage of the mountain range, we went
ahead so fast that I had little opportunity,
even if I had the enterprise, to look among
the few prisoners for the circus-rider.

Time passed, and we were at the end of a
three days' fight near Philippopolis, in the
middle of January. Suleiman Pasha's army,
defeated, disorganized, and at last disband-
ed, though to that day still unconquered,
had finished the tragic act of its last campaign with the heroic stand made in the
foot-hills of the Rhodope Mountains, near
Stanimaka, south of Philippopolis. A long
month in the terrible cold, on the summits
of the Balkan range; the forced retreat
through the snow after the battle of Tasko-
sen; the neck-and-neck race with the Russians down the valley of the Maritza; finally,

the hot little battle on the river-bank, and the two days of hand-to-hand struggle in the vineyards of Stanimaka—this was a campaign to break the constitution of any soldier. Days without food, nights without shelter from the mountain blasts, always marching and always fighting, supplies and baggage lost, ammunition and artillery gone—human nature could hold out no longer, and the Turkish army dissolved away into the defiles of the Rhodopes. Unfortunately for her, Turkey has no literature to chronicle, no art to perpetuate, the heroism of her defenders.

The incidents of that short campaign are too full of horror to be related. Not only did the demon of war devour strong men, but found dainty morsels for its bloody maw in innocent women and children. Whole families, crazed by the belief that capture was worse than death, fought in the ranks with the soldiers. Women, ambushed in coverts, shot the Russians as they rummaged the captured trains for much-needed food. Little children, thrown into the snow by the flying parents, died of cold and starvation,

8

or were trampled to death by passing caval-
ry. Such a useless waste of human life has
not been recorded since the indiscriminate
massacres of the Middle Ages.

The sight of human suffering soon blunts
the sensibilities of any one who lives with
it, so that he is at last able to look upon it
with no stronger feeling than that of help-
lessness. Resigned to the inevitable, he is
no longer impressed by the woes of the individual. He looks upon the illness, wounds,
and death of the soldier as a part of the lot
of all combatants, and comes to consider
him an insignificant unit of the great mass
of men. At last, only novelties in horrors
will excite his feelings.

I was riding back from the Stanimaka battle-field, sufficiently elated at the prospect of
a speedy termination of the war—now made
certain by the breaking-up of Suleiman's
army—to forget where I was, and to imagine
myself back in my comfortable apartments in
Paris. I only awoke from my dream at the
station where the highway from Stanimaka
crosses the railway line about a mile south

of Philippopolis. The great wooden bar-
racks had been used as a hospital for wounded Turks, and, as I drew up my horse at the
door, the last of the lot of four hundred, who
had been starving there nearly a week, were
being placed upon carts to be transported
to the town. The road to Philippopolis was
crowded with wounded and refugees. Peas-
ant families struggled along with all their
household goods piled upon a single cart.
Ammunition wagons and droves of cattle,
rushing along against the tide of human be-
ings towards the distant bivouacs, made the
confusion hopeless. Night was fast coming
on, and, in company with a Cossack, who
was, like myself, seeking the headquarters of
General Gourko, I made my way through the
tangle of men, beasts, and wagons in the direction of the town. It was one of those chill,
wet days of winter when there is little comfort away from a blazing fire, and when good
shelter for the night is an absolute necessity.
The drizzle had saturated my garments, and
the snow-mud had soaked my boots. Sharp
gusts of piercing wind drove the cold mist

along, and as the temperature fell in the late afternoon, the slush of the roads began to stiffen and the fog froze where it gathered. Every motion of the limbs seemed to expose some unprotected part of the body to the cold and wet. No amount of exercise that was possible with stiffened limbs and in wet garments would warm the blood. Leading my horse, I splashed along, holding my arms away from my body, and only moving my benumbed fingers to wipe the chill drip from my face. It was weather to take the courage out of the strongest man, and the sight of the soaked and shivering wounded, packed in the jolting carts or limping through the mud, gave me, hardened as I was, a painful contraction of the heart. The best I could do was to lift upon my worn-out horse one brave young fellow who was hobbling along with a bandaged leg. Followed by the Cossack, whose horse bore a similar burden, I hurried along, hoping to get under cover before dark. At the entrance to the town numerous camp-fires burned in the bivouacs of the refugees, who were huddled together in the shelter of their wagons, trying to warm themselves in the smoke of the wet fuel. I could see the wounded, as they were jolted past in the heavy carts, look longingly at the kettles of boiling maize which made the evening meal of the houseless natives.

Inside the town, the wounded and the refugees were still more miserable than those we had passed on the way. Loaded carts blocked the streets. Every house was occupied, and the narrow sidewalks were crowded with Russian soldiers, who looked wretched enough in their dripping overcoats, as they stamped their rag-swathed feet. At the corner, in front of the great Khan, motley groups of Greeks, Bulgarians, and Russians were gathered, listlessly watching the line of hobbling wounded as they turned the corner to find their way among the carts, up the hill to the hospital, near the Konak. By the time I reached the Khan the Cossack who accompanied me had fallen behind in the confusion, and, without waiting for him, I pushed along, wading in the gutter, dragging

my horse by the bridle. Half-way up the
hill I saw a crowd of natives watching with
curiosity two Russian guardsmen and a Turkish prisoner. The latter was evidently exhausted, for he was crouching in the freezing
mud of the street. , Presently the soldiers
shook him roughly, and raised him forcibly
to his feet, and, half supporting him between
them, they moved slowly along, the Turk
balancing on his stiffened legs, and swinging
from side to side.

He was a most wretched object to look at.
He had neither boots nor fez ; his feet were
bare, and his trousers were torn off near the
knee, and hung in tatters around his mud-
splashed legs. An end of the red sash fastened to his waist trailed far behind in the
mud. A blue-cloth jacket hung loosely from
his shoulders, and his hands and wrists dan-
gled from the ragged sleeves. His head
rolled around at each movement of the
body, and at short intervals the muscles of
the neck would rigidly contract. All at once
he drew himself up with a shudder and sank
down in the mud again.

The guardsmen were themselves near the end of their strength, and their patience was well-nigh finished as well. Rough mountain marching had torn the soles from their boots, and great, unsightly wraps of raw-hide and rags were bound on their feet. The thin, worn overcoats, burned in many places, flapped dismally against their ankles; and their caps, beaten out of shape by many storms, clung drenched to their heads. They were in no condition to help any one to walk, for they could scarcely get on alone. They stood a moment shivering, looked at each other, shook their heads as if discouraged, and proceeded to rouse the Turk by hauling him upon his feet again. The three moved on a few yards, and the prisoner fell again, and the same operation was repeated. All this time I was crowding nearer and nearer, and as I got within a half-dozen paces, the Turk fell once more, and this time lay at full length in the mud. The guardsmen tried to rouse him by shaking, but in vain. Finally, one of them, losing all patience, pricked him with his bayonet on the lower part of the

ribs exposed by the raising of the jacket as
he fell. I was now near enough to act, and
with a sudden clutch I pulled the guardsman
away, whirled him around, and stood in his
place. As I was stooping over the Turk he
raised himself slowly, doubtless aroused by
the pain of the puncture, and turned on me
a most beseeching look, which changed at
once into something like joy and surprise.
Immediately a death-like pallor spread over
his face, and he sank back again with a groan.

By this time quite a crowd of Bulgarians
had gathered around us, and seemed to enjoy
the sight of a suffering enemy. It was evident that they did not intend to volunteer
any assistance, so I helped the wounded
Russian down from my saddle, and invited
the natives rather sternly to put the Turk in
his place. With true Bulgarian spirit they
refused to assist a Turk, and it required the
argument of the raw-hide (*nagajka*) to bring
them to their senses. Three of them, cornered and flogged, lifted the unconscious
man and carried him towards the horse; the
soldiers meanwhile, believing me to be an

officer, standing in the attitude of attention.
As the Bulgarians bore the Turk to the
horse, a few drops of blood fell to the
ground. I noticed then that he had his
shirt tied around his left shoulder, under his
jacket. Supported in the saddle by two
natives on each side, his head falling forward
on his breast, the wounded prisoner was carried with all possible tenderness to the Staf-
ford House Hospital, near the Konak. As
we moved slowly up the hill, I looked back,
and saw the two guardsmen sitting on the
muddy sidewalk, with their guns leaning
against their shoulders—too much exhausted to go either way.

I found room for my charge in one of the
upper rooms of the hospital, where he was
washed and put into a warm bed. His
wound proved to be a severe one. A Ber-
dan bullet had passed through the thick part
of the left pectoral, out again, and into the
head of the humerus. The surgeon said
that the arm would have to be operated on,
to remove the upper quarter of the bone.

The next morning I went to the hospital

to see what had become of the wounded
man, for the incident of the previous evening had made a deep impression on my mind.
As I walked through the corridor I saw a
group around a temporary bed in the corner.
Some one was evidently about to undergo
an operation, for an assistant held at intervals a great cone of linen over a haggard
face on the pillow, and a strong smell of
chloroform filled the air. As I approached,
the surgeon turned around, and, recognizing
me, said with a nod and a smile, "We are at
work on your friend." While he was speaking, he bared the left shoulder of the wounded man, and I saw the holes made by the
bullet as it passed from the pectoral into the
upper part of the deltoid. Without waiting longer, the surgeon made a straight cut
downward from near the acromion through
the thick fibre of the deltoid to the bone.
He attempted to sever the tendons so as to
slip the head of the humerus from the socket,
but failed. He wasted no time in further trial,
but made a second incision from the bullet-
hole diagonally to the middle of the first cut,

and turned the pointed flap up over the shoulder. It was now easy to unjoint the bones, and but a moment's work to saw off the shattered piece of the humerus, tie the severed arteries, and bring the flap again into its place.

There was no time to pause, for the surgeon began to fear the effects of the chloroform on the patient. We hastened to revive him by every possible means at hand, throwing cold water on him and warming his hands and feet. Although under the influence of chloroform to the degree that he was insensible to pain, he had not been permitted to lose his entire consciousness, and he appeared to be sensible of what we were doing. Nevertheless, he awoke slowly, very slowly, the surgeon meanwhile putting the stitches in the incision. At last he raised his eyelids, made a slight movement with his lips, and then deliberately surveyed the circle of faces gathered closely around the bed. There was something in his eyes which had an irresistible attraction for me, and I bent forward to intercept his gaze.

As his eyes met mine they changed as if a
sudden light had struck them, and the stony
stare gave way to a look of intelligence and
recognition.   Then, through the beard of a
season's growth, and behind the haggard
mask before me, I saw at once the circus-
rider of Turin and Paris.   I remember being
scarcely excited or surprised at the meeting,
for a great sense of irresponsibility came
over me, and I involuntarily accepted the
coincidence as a matter of course.   He tried
in vain to speak, but held up his right hand
and feebly made with his fingers the sign of
the letter which had played such an important part in the story of his life.   Even at that
instant the light left his eyes, and something
like a veil seemed drawn over them.   With
the instinctive energy which possesses every
one when there is a chance of saving human life, we redoubled our efforts to restore
the patient to consciousness.   But while we
strove to feed the flame with some of our
own vitality, it flickered and went out, leaving the hue of ashes where the rosy tinge of
life had been.   His heart was paralyzed.

As I turned away, my eye caught the surgeon's incision, which was now plainly visible
on the left shoulder. The cut was in the
form of the letter Y.

TEDESCO'S RUBINA

TEDESCO'S RUBINA

A NY one may see among the fragments of antique sculpture in one of the museums of Rome a marble head of a young maiden which has been rudely broken off at the neck. It bears no marks of restoration, and is mounted on the conventional pedestal or support. There is a half-coquettish twinkle in the lines of the mouth and eyes, and a most bewitching expression of innocent youthful happiness about the face, which at once attract and fascinate the eye of even the most careless observer of these relics of ancient art. The head is gracefully poised and exquisitely proportioned, but is not conventionalized to the degree usual in busts of a similar character. Indeed, notwithstanding its classical aspect, there is a marked individuality of treatment noticeable

9

in its composition, if I may so call the arrangement of the hair and the pose of the
head.   The features are small and regular;
the chin a trifle too delicate, if possible, to
complete the full oval suggested by the upper part of the face; and the hair, in which a
wreath of ivy is twined, clusters in slender,
irregular curls around a low forehead, and is
gathered behind in a loose knot.   One tress
of hair, escaping from the embrace of the
ivy - branch, caressingly clings to the neck.
On the pedestal is the label:

"A Roman Nymph—Fragment."

Visiting the museum one day in company
with two artist friends, I pointed this head
out to them as we were hastily passing
through the room.   Like myself, they were
enchanted with the fragment, and lingered
to sketch it.   They were very long in making their sketches; and after they declared
them finished, shut their books with a reso-
lute air, walked briskly off, but returned
again, one after the other, to take another
look.   At last I succeeded in dragging them

away; but while we were examining another part of the collection, in an adjoining room, each disappeared in turn, and came back, after a few minutes' absence, with the volunteered excuse that he had found it necessary to put a last touch on his drawing of the attractive fragment. When we left the museum both of my infatuated friends had made arrangements with the custodian to permit a moulder to come and take a cast of the head.

The island of Capri is the most delightful spot in the Mediterranean. Blessed with a fine climate, a comparatively fertile soil, and a contented population, it is one of the best places accessible to the ordinary traveller in which to spend a quiet season. In this refuge life does not sparkle, but stagnates. Tired nerves recover their tone in the eventless succession of lazy days. Overtaxed digestion regains its normal strength through the simple diet, the pure air, and the repose of mind and body which are found in this paradise. Of late years the island has become a great resort for artists of all nationalities. Many good studios are to be had there; plenty of trained models of both sexes and all ages are eager to work for trifling wages; living is cheap, rents are by no means exorbitant, and subjects for pictures abound at every step.

A few modern buildings of some pretensions to size and architectural style have been erected within the last twenty or thirty years, but the greater part of the houses on the island, both in the town of Capri and in the village of Anacapri, are very old and exceedingly simple in construction. The streets of the town are narrow and crooked, and twist about in a perfect maze of tufa walls and whitewashed façades, straggling away in all directions from the piazza. The dwellings of the poorer classes are jumbled together along these narrow streets as if space were very valuable. They overhang and even span the roadway at intervals, and frequently the flat roof of one house serves as a *loggia*, or broad balcony, for the one above it. Small gardens are sometimes cultivated on these housetops, and the bleating of goats and cackling of hens are often heard in the shrubbery there. Not the least among the many attractions of Capri are its historical relics. Ruined Roman villas and palaces abound all over the hills; traces of ancient baths and grottos of the nymphs may be seen along the water's edge; and fragments of Roman architecture are built into every wall, and into almost every house. The peculiar geological formation of the island furnishes the excuse for a variety of short and pleasant excursions; for there are numbers of interesting caves, strange rock forms, and grandly picturesque cliffs and cañons within easy reach by sea or by land.

When I was in Capri, there was one remarkably pretty girl among the models, called Lisa. She was only fifteen years old, but, like the usual type of Southern maiden, was as fully developed as if she were three or four years older. Her father and mother were dead, and she lived with her great-grandmother in a small house of a single room in a narrow street which ran directly under my bedroom. None of the houses of the quarter where my studio and apartment were situated had glass in the windows, but the interiors were lighted, like those of the ancient Romans, by square holes provided with wooden shutters. From the rude window in my bedroom, and also from the *loggia* in front of the studio, I could look directly down into the small dwelling below, and at all times of the day could see the old woman knitting in the shadow just inside the open door, and Lisa flitting about, busy with the primitive housekeeping. Whenever I wanted the girl to sit for me, I had only to call down and she would come up to the studio. It takes but a few days to become intimately acquainted with the simple-hearted islanders, and in a short time the old woman grew very friendly and communicative. At my invitation she frequently came to sit on the *loggia*, whence she could look over the sea, towards the south, to watch for returning coral fishermen, or on the other side, to the north and east, where Naples shimmered in the sun, and Vesuvius reared its sombre cone. She was not comely to

look upon, for she was wrinkled beyond belief, and her parchment skin was the color of
oak-tanned leather. She often said that
Lisa was the image of her own family, but I
could trace no resemblance between the
blooming maid and the withered dame.
The chief beauty of the young girl's face, or
at least the most remarkable feature of it,
was the eyes, which were of a deep-blue
gray, almost as brilliant as the rich, dark
ones common to the Italian type, but more
unique and more charming in contrast with
the olive-tinted skin and black hair. The
old woman's eyes were as dark as those of
the generality of her race, and apparently
but little dimmed by her great age. All
over the island she had the reputation of
being the oldest inhabitant; but as she could
not remember the date of her birth — if, indeed, she ever knew it — and as there had
been no records kept at the time she was
born, there was no means of proving the
truth or the falsity of the tales about her
wonderful age. She bore everywhere the
peculiar name of La Rubina di Tedesco—

Tedesco's Rubina—the significance of which, although it was variously explained by common tradition, had really been forgotten more than a generation before, and was now known only to herself. The islanders are fond of giving nicknames, and I should not have remarked this one among so many others if it had not been for the word Tedesco, which in Italian means German. My curiosity was excited on this account, to discover what the name really meant and why it had been given to her.

In the long summer twilights I used to talk with the old woman by the hour, or rather I used to listen to her by the hour, for without a word of encouragement from me she would drone on in her queer patois in the garrulous way very old people have, elaborating the details of the most trivial incidents, and rehearsing the intimate family history of all her numerous acquaintances, She looked upon me with the more favor because it happened that I was the only artist who employed Lisa, and consequently furnished all the money for the support of

the small household.   Relying on the position I held in her esteem as patron, and can-
nily increasing her obligation to me by various small presents, I schemed for a long time
to make her tell the history of her own life.
She had an aggravating way of either utterly
ignoring all questions on this subject, or else
of taking refuge in a series of wails on the
change in the times and on the degeneracy
of the islanders.   By degrees and at long intervals I did, however, succeed in getting a
full account of her early life and of the origin of her popular name.

Long ago, even long before any steamers
were seen on the Bay of Naples, two young
Germans—a sculptor and an architect—wandered down to Capri, to study the antiquities of the island.   They were both capti-
vated by the beauties of the spot, by the de-
lights of the pastoral life they led there, and
possibly also by the charms of the island
maidens, who even then had a wide reputation for beauty, and they consequently stayed
on indefinitely.   Rubina was then a girl of
fourteen, and held the enviable position of

belle of Anacapri. The sculptor, whose name was Carl Deutsch, somehow made the acquaintance of the beauty, and after a time persuaded her to sit to him. He first made a bust in wax, and then began to work it out in marble, using for his material an antique block found in one of the ruined palaces of Tiberius. Days and weeks he toiled over this bust, and as he worked he grew hopelessly in love with his model. As time passed, the islanders, with their usual freedom with foreigners' names, translated Carl Deutsch into its Italian equivalent, Carlo Tedesco, and Rubina, who was constantly employed by the sculptor as a model, was naturally called Tedesco's Rubina.

Then on the peaceful island was enacted the same old tragedy that has been played all over the world myriads of times before and since. Tedesco's friend, the architect, also fell in love with the model, and took advantage of the sculptor's preoccupation with his work to gain the girl's affection. Early in the morning, while his friend was engaged in preparing his clay and arranging his stu-

dio for the day, he would toil up the six hundred stone steps which led to the village of
Anacapri, on the plateau above, meet Rubina, and accompany her down as far as the
outskirts of the town.   Then often, at the
close of the day, when the sculptor, oppressed
with the hopeless feeling of discouragement
and despair which at times comes over every
true artist, would give up his favorite stroll
with Rubina and remain to gaze at his work
and ponder over it, the architect would be
sure to take his place.   So it went on to the
usual climax.   Rubina, flattered by the as-
siduous attentions of the one, and somewhat
piqued by the frequent fits of absent-mind-
edness and preoccupation of the other, at
last reluctantly gave her consent to marry
the architect, who planned an elopement
without exciting a suspicion on the part of
the sculptor that his idol was stolen from
him.   The faithless friend, pretending to the
innocent girl that, being of different relig-
ions, it was necessary for them to go to the
mainland to be married, sailed away with her
one morning at daybreak without the knowl-

edge of any one save the two men who were
hired to row them to Naples. Where they
went, and how long they lived together, I
could not find out, for she would not open
her lips about that portion of her history.
Only after a great deal of persuasive interro-
gation did I learn that when she came back
she brought with her a girl baby a few
months old. It was always believed in the
village that her husband had died. I drew
my own inference about the circumstances
of her return.

When she reached the island, Tedesco had
long since disappeared, and, although there
were no absolute proofs, he was thought to
be dead. For months after he had learned
of the faithlessness of both sweetheart and
friend he had been seen very little outside his
studio. What he did there was not known,
for he invited nobody to enter. Even the
neighbor's wife who had done the housekeeping for the two young men did not see
the interior of the studio after Rubina ran
away. She gossiped of the sculptor to the
women down the street, and they all shook

their heads, touched their foreheads signifi-
cantly with index-fingers, and sadly repeated,
"*Un po' matto, un po' matto*" — "A little
mad." Several weeks passed after the flight
of the young couple, and then the sculptor
was observed nearly every morning to walk
over one of the hills in the direction of a
high cliff. Sometimes he was absent but a
few hours, but on other days he did not return until night. At length, towards the end
of winter, he gave up his studio and apartment without a word of his plans to any one.
When he had departed, carrying the few articles of clothing which were kept in the
outer room, the housekeeper entered the
studio and found, to her astonishment, that,
with the sculptor, all traces of his work had
disappeared.

After a while it was discovered that he had
taken up his abode in a certain cave near the
water's edge, at the foot of the cliff, along
the top of which he had been frequently seen
walking. This cave had always been considered approachable only from the water
side; but some men who were fishing for

cuttlefish near the shore had seen the mad
sculptor clamber down the precipice and enter the mouth of the cave, which was half
closed by accumulated rubble and sand. . The
fishermen, of course, exaggerated their story,
and the simple islanders, who always regard
a demented person with awe, came to believe that the sculptor possessed superhu-
man strength and agility; and, although their
curiosity concerning his mode of life and occupation was much excited, their superstitious fears prevented them from interfering
with him or attempting to investigate his actions. At long intervals the hermit would
appear in the piazza, receive his letters, buy
a few articles of food, and disappear again,
not to be seen for weeks.

Summer passed and a second winter came
on, and with it a succession of unusually severe storms. During one of these long gales
the sea rose several feet, and the breakers
beat against the rocks with terrific force. On
the weather side of the island all the boats
which had not been hauled up much higher
than usual were dashed to pieces. No one

dared to leave the island, and there was no
communication with the mainland for nearly
two weeks. After that storm the sculptor was
never seen again. Some fishermen ventured
into the mouth of the cave, now washed clear
of rubbish, but discovered nothing. It was
therefore believed that the hermit, with all
his belongings, was swept out to sea by the
waves. Of late years no one had visited the
cave, because the military guard stationed near
by to prevent the people from gathering salt
on the rocks, and thus evading the payment
of the national tax on this article, had pro-
hibited boats from landing there. This pro-
hibition was strengthened by the orders which
forbade the exploration of any of the Roman
ruins or grottos on the island by persons not
employed for that purpose by the government. Several years before, the authorities
had examined all the ruins. They had carried to Naples all the antiquities they could
find, and then had put a penalty on the ex-
plorations of the islanders, to whom the antiquities are popularly supposed to belong
by right of inheritance. This regulation had

created a great deal of bad feeling, particularly since several peasants had been fined
and imprisoned for simply digging up a few
relics to sell to travellers.

I asked the old woman what became of
her child, for she did not readily volunteer
any information concerning her.

"*Ah, signor padrone,*" she said, " she was
a perfect little German, with hair as blond
as the fleece of the yellow goats.   She was a
good child, but was never very strong.   She
married a coral fisherman when she was seventeen, and died giving birth to Lisa's mother.   Poor thing! May the blessed Maria,
mother of God, rest her soul!   Lisa's mother
was blond also, but with hair like the flame
of sunset.   She was a fine, strong creature,
and could carry a sack of salt up the steps
to Anacapri as well as any girl in the village
—yes, even better than any other.   She married a custom-house officer and moved to Naples, where she had meat on her table once
every blessed week.   But even in her pros-
perity the misfortunes of the family followed
her, and the cholera carried off her husband,

herself, and a boy baby—may their souls rest
in Paradise!—leaving Lisa alone in the world
but for me, who have lived to see all this
misery and all these changes. Father, Son,
and Holy Ghost! Lisa resembles her mother
only in her eyes. All the rest of her is Ca-
prian. Ah me! ah me! She's the image of
what I was, except her eyes. By the grace
of God I am able to see it! May the Virgin spare her to suffer—" and so on to the
end of the chapter of mingled family history
and invocations.

Lisa resemble her? I thought. Impossible. What! that wrinkled skin ever know
the bloom of youth like that on Lisa's cheek;
that sharp chin ever have a rounded contour;
that angular face ever show as perfect an
oval as the one fringed by the wavy hair
straggling out from Lisa's kerchief? Did
that mask, seared with the marks of years of
suffering, privation, and toil, ever bear the
sweet, bewitching expression which in Lisa's
face haunts me with a vague, half-remem-
bered fascination? Never! It cannot be!

This history of a love-tragedy, enacted when

10

Goethe was still walking among the artificial
antiquities in the groves of Weimar had a
curious charm for me. I patiently listened
to hours of irrelevant gossip and uninteresting description of family matters before I
succeeded in getting together even as meagre a thread of the story as the one I have
just repeated. The old woman had a feeble
memory for recent events and dates, but she
seemed to be able to recollect as well as ever
incidents which took place at the beginning
of the century. She retailed the scandals of
fifty years ago with as much delight as if the
interested parties had not all of them long
since been followed to the hillside graveyard
or been buried in the waste of waters in that
mysterious region known as the coral fisheries.

Partly in order to test the accuracy of her
memory, and partly to satisfy my curiosity,
I persuaded her to show me the place where
the sculptor used to walk along the edge of
the cliff. I had previously taken a look at
the cave from the water, and knew its position in relation to the cliff, but had never
been able to discover how the German had

succeeded in clambering up and down. Accordingly, one Sunday afternoon, when most of the islanders were in church, she hobbled along with me a short distance up the hillside and pointed out the spot where the children had seen the mad sculptor vanish in the air. This place was marked by a projecting piece of rock, which cropped out of the turf on the very edge of the cliff, not at its highest point, but at some distance down the shoulder of the hill, where it had been broken sheer off in the great convulsion of nature which raised the isolated, lofty island above the sea. I could not induce her to go within a dozen rods or more of the edge of the cliff, and, having shown me the spot I wished to find, she hobbled homeward again.

There was no path across the hill in any direction, and the scant grass was rarely trodden except by the goats and their keepers. On that Sunday forenoon there was no one in sight except, a long distance off, a shepherd watching a few goats. Thinking it a favorable opportunity to investigate the truth of the story about the sculptor, I walked up to the very brink of the precipice and lay down flat on the top of the piece of rock pointed out by the old woman, and cautiously looked over the abyss. The cliff below me was by no means sheer, for it was broken by a number of irregular shelf-like projections, a few inches wide, upon which loose bits of falling stone had caught from time to time. Cautiously looking over the cliff, I saw at once that it would be possible for me to let myself down to the first irregular projection, or bench, provided I could get some firm hold for my hands. The turf afforded no such hold, and at the very edge, where it was crumbled by the weather, it was so broken as to be dangerous to stand on. I looked along the smooth, perpendicular ledge, but found no ring to fasten a rope to and no marks of any such contrivance. A careful search in the immediate neighborhood disclosed no signs of a wooden post or stake, or, indeed, anything which would serve as an anchor for a hand rope. I lay down and hung over the cliff, to see if I could discover any traces of a ladder, marks of spikes, tell-tale streaks of iron-rust, or anything to show how the descent had been made. Nothing of the kind was visible.

Far below, the great expanse of turquoise sea, stained with the shadows of summer clouds, seemed to rise with a convex surface to meet the sky at the distant horizon line. Away off to the south, towards Stromboli and Sicily, a few sails, minute white dots relieved against the delicate blue water, hung motionless, as if suspended in an opalescent ether. To the left the green shores of the mainland stretched away to hazy Pæstum. To the right the headland of Anacapri rose majestically against the tender summer sky, and a bank of cumulus clouds was reflected in the smooth sea. Beneath screamed a flock of sea-gulls, sailing hither and thither in graceful flight.

While dreaming over the beauty of the scene before me, I suddenly caught sight out of the very corner of my eye, as it were, of a crevice in the ledge beside me, almost hidden by the grass which grew tall against the rock. Hastily tearing the grass away with my right hand, I found that this cleft, which was only a couple of inches wide at the most, continued downward along the face of the cliff in a slanting direction, rapidly diminishing in width until it lost itself or became a simple crack in the rock. With my knife and fingers I dug the cleft out clean, as far in as I could reach, expecting to find an iron rod or a spike or something to which a rope could be fastened. But I was again disappointed, for there were no signs of iron and no visible marks of man's handiwork. Whether this was an artificial excavation in the rock, or merely an accidental irregularity, I could not determine, but it made a perfect hold for the hand, like an inverted draw-pull. The moment I discovered this I saw how the descent could easily be accomplished, and without stopping to reflect I clutched my right hand firmly in the cleft and swung off the cliff. My feet struck a pile of loose stones, but I soon kicked them off, made a solid foothold for myself, and then cautiously turned around. The wall of rock pitched backward sufficiently for me to lean up against it, with my face to the sea, and stand there perfectly secure. When I turned again and stood facing the rock, my head was above the edge of the cliff so that I could overlook quite an area of the hilltop. Before attempting to descend the cliff I thought it prudent to test my ability to reach the turf again. Seizing the cleft with the fingers of my right hand, and clutching the irregularities of the edge of the rock with my left, I easily swung myself upon my chest, and then upon my knees, and stood on the turf. Elated now by my success, I let myself over the edge again, and began the difficult task of picking my way down the face of the cliff. By diligently kicking and pushing the rubble from the bench I was on, I slowly made my way along, steadying myself as well as I could by putting my fingers in the crevices of the rock. In two places I found three or four holes, which had the appearance of having been artificially made, and by the aid of these I let myself down to the second and third projecting benches. From this point the descent was made without much difficulty, although I carefully refrained from casting my eyes seaward during the whole climb. Fortunately I was on the face of the cliff, which was at a receding angle, and consequently was not swept by the telescope of the guard on the beach to the right, and I finished the descent and reached a point to the left of the mouth of the cave, and on a level with it, without any interruption. I was too much fatigued to care to risk discovery by the guard in entering the cave, which was in full sight of his station; so, after resting awhile on the rocks, I clambered up the path I had come, and found that the ascent, though toilsome, was not particularly difficult.

I told no one of my adventure, not even the old woman; but early the next Sunday morning I went down the cliff again, unobserved as before, and, watching my chance when the guard was sweeping the shore to the right with his glass, I stole into the cave. It was an irregular hole, perhaps thirty feet deep at its greatest length, and not over ten feet high in any part. Three shallow, alcove-like chambers led off the main room. These

were all three nearly full of gravel, sand, and
disintegrated rock, and the floor of the whole
cavern was covered with this same accumulation.   There were plentiful marks of the
labors of the Italian antiquarians, for the
ground had all been dug up, and the last
shallow pits which had been excavated to
the bed-rock had not been refilled.

With no settled purpose I took up a piece
of an old spade I found there, and began to
dig on one side of the cave near the largest
alcove.   The accumulation was not packed
hard, and I easily threw it aside.   I had re-
moved a few feet of earth without finding
anything to reward my labors, and then began to dig in the heap of rubbish which was
piled in the alcove, nearly touching its low
ceiling.   Almost the first shovelful of earth
I threw out had a number of small gray tesseræ in it.   Gathering these up and taking
them to the light, I found that part of them
were of marble, or other light-colored stone ;
but that a few were of glass with a corroded
surface, which could be clipped off with great
ease, disclosing beautiful iridescent cubes un-

derneath. The whole day was passed in this
work, for I was much interested in my discovery. The tesseræ were of no great value,
to be sure, but they proved that the cave had
been used by the Romans, probably as a
grotto of the nymphs, and they were certain-
ly worth keeping in a private collection. Possibly not a little of the charm of the operation of excavating was due to the element of
danger in it. The guard was stationed less
than a ·rifle-shot away, and if I had been
discovered, fine and possibly imprisonment
would have been my lot.

To make a long story short, I made several
excursions to the cave in the same manner,
and dug nearly the whole ground in a sys-
tematic way, leaving until the last a small alcove near the mouth of the cave, because I
found very few tesseræ anywhere in the
strong daylight. Everything which was not
a simple, uninteresting piece of stone or shell
I stowed away in a bag and carried to my
studio. In a few Sundays I had a peck or
more of tesseræ, a quarter of them glass
ones, and a great many bits of twisted glass

rod and small pieces of glass vessels. One
day the spade turned out, among other
things, several small pieces of brown, porous
substance which looked in the dim light like
decayed wood. I put them in the bag with
the rest, to be examined at my leisure at
home. The next morning, when I came to
turn out the collection gathered the day before, these curious pieces fell out with the
rest, and immediately attracted my attention. In the strong light of day, I saw at
once what they were. They were the decayed phalanges of a human hand. The story
of Tedesco and Rubina was always in my
mind; and I compared the bones with my
own fingers, and found them to be without
doubt the bones of an adult, and probably
of a man.

I could scarcely wait for the next Sunday
to arrive, but I did not dare to risk the descent of the cliff on a week-day lest I should
be seen by the fishermen. When at last I
did reach the cave again, I went at my work
with vigor, continuing my search in the place
where I left off the previous week. In a short

time I unearthed several more bones similar
to those I already had, but, although I thoroughly examined every cubic foot of earth
which I had not previously dug over, I found
no more of the skeleton.

In my studio that evening I arranged the
little bones as well as I could in the positions
they had occupied in the human hand. As
far as I could make out, I had the thumb,
the first and third fingers and one joint of
the second, three of the bones of the hand,
and one of the wrist-bones. There could be
no question but these had once belonged to
a human hand, and to the right hand, too.
There was no means of knowing how long
ago the person had died, neither could there
be any possible way of identifying these
human relics. The possession of the grew-
some little objects seemed to set my imagination on fire. After going to bed at night
I often worked myself into a state of disagreeable nervous tension by meditating on
the history of the sculptor, and revolving in
my mind the theories I had formed of the
mystery of his life and the manner of his

death. For some reason the old woman had never told me where his studio had been, and it never occurred to me to ask her until the thought suddenly came during one of these night-hours of wakefulness. When I put the question to her the next afternoon, she replied, simply:

"This studio was his, *signor padrone*."

The poor old soul had been living her life over again, day after day, as she sat knitting and looking out to sea, her imagination quickened and her memory refreshed by the surroundings which in many decades had scarcely changed at all.

This information gave a new stimulus to my thoughts, and I lay awake and pondered and surmised more than ever. There seemed to be something hidden away in my own consciousness, which was endeavoring to work its way into recognition. It would almost come in range of my mental vision, and then would lose itself again, just as some well-known name will coquettishly elude the grasp of the memory. While lying awake in a real agony of thought, a vague feeling would en-

ter my mind for an instant, that I had only
to interpret what I already knew, and the
mystery of my imagination would be clear
to me. Then I would revolve and revolve
again all the details of the story, but the fugi-
tive idea always escaped me. With that discouraging persistence which is utterly beyond
our control, whenever great anxiety weighs
upon our minds, I would repeat, again and
again, the same series of arguments and the
same line of theories until at last, utterly
worn out, I would go to sleep. It was quite
inexplicable that I should think so much
about a sculptor of whom I had never heard,
except from Tedesco's Rubina, and who died
long before I was born; but, in spite of my
reason, I could not rid myself of the vague
consciousness that there was something I was
unwittingly hiding from myself.

One warm night in summer I sat up quite
late writing letters, and then, thinking I
should go to sleep at once on account of my
fatigue, went to bed. But sleep came only
after some hours, and even then not until I
had stood for a long time looking out of the

window on the moonlit houses below, with
my bare feet on the cold stone floor. The
first thought that came to my head, as I
awoke the next morning, was about that
marble head I had seen in Rome a year before. The dark page of my mind became
illuminated in an instant. I did not need to
summon Lisa to note the resemblance of her
face to the marble one which had so fasci-
nated me, for I was familiar enough with her
features to require no aid to my memory.
Besides, I had a fairly accurate study of her
head on my easel, and I compared the face
on the canvas with the marble one which I
now remembered so vividly. There was the
identical contour of the cheeks and forehead,
with the hyper-delicate chin; the nose, the
mouth, the eyes, each repeated the forms of
the marble bust. It was the color alone
that gave the painting its modern aspect, and
it had been, I now saw, my preoccupation
with the color which had prevented my observing the resemblance before. The only
thing my portrait lacked, as a representa-
tion of the model from whom the marble was

made, was that fascinating expression of
girlhood, which, I was obliged to confess
to myself, I had not succeeded in catching.

Full of my discovery, I wrote at once to
the authorities in Rome, asking for a history
of the fragment.

In a few days I received the not unexpected information that it had been given by
the Naples Museum in exchange for another
piece of antique sculpture. I hurried across
to Naples and interviewed the authorities
there, requesting precise statements about
the bust, on the plea that I was interested in
the particular period of art which it represented. In the list of objects of antiquity
excavated in the summer of 18—, I found
this entry, under the head of Capri:

"Female head with ivy wreath in hair—
Marble—Broken off at neck—No other fragments discovered. Mem.: This probably belonged to a statue of a sea-nymph, as it was
found in a grotto with the remains of mosaic
pavement and ceiling."

In return for this information I gave the

authorities my sincere thanks, but not my secret.

Three years later I met my two artist friends in New York. Like all who have torn themselves away from the enchanting influences of Italy, we reviewed with delight every incident of our sojourn there, not forgetting the visit to the museum in Rome. Two plaster copies of the head had been made, and the mould then broken.

In each of the studios the plaster head occupied the place of honor, and its owner exhausted the choicest terms of art phraseology in its praise. Foolish fellows, they could not escape from the potent spell of its bewitching expression, and, burdened with the weight of the sentimental secret, each of them took occasion, privately and with great hesitation and shamefacedness, to confess to me that he had stolen away, while we were together in the museum in Rome, to kiss the marble lips of the fascinating fragment.

To each of them I made the same remark:

11

" My dear fellow, if you were so foolish as to fall in love with a marble head, and a fragment at that, what would you have done in my place? I was intimately acquainted with the model who sat for it!"

MEDUSA'S HEAD

MEDUSA'S HEAD

H ENRY SEYMOUR fancied he was a
realist.   Indeed, he was very much
annoyed when his work was described by an
art critic as idealistic, or when he was allud-
ed to in the art columns as " a rising young
artist quite out of place in the realistic circle
to which he affects to belong."   But the bias
of mind which prevented him from recognizing the real qualities in his own productions,
equally hindered him from accomplishing
what was his present highest ambition — an
accurate and realistic imitation of nature.
In common with the large majority of the
young artists of the day, he studied two or
three years in Europe, notably in Paris,
where he learned to believe, or fancied he
believed, that the most hopeful tendency of
modern art consisted in the elimination of

all idea and all sentiment from the motive
of a picture, and the glorification of the
naturalistic and, if I may say so, earthly
qualities of the model.

After his return from the ateliers of Paris,
Seymour divided his time between the
apotheosis of rags and squalor and the de-
lineation of the features of the New York
banker, broker, or insurance president, with
an occasional excursion into the field of female portraiture, which was opened to him
through the large and influential circle of
friends and acquaintances of his family.
His efforts in this direction frequently resulted in popular and artistic success, and
after a season or two gained for him a profitable and exceedingly agreeable line of sitters. A strange jumble of millionaires, boot-
blacks, society ladies, and beggar-women
covered the canvases that encumbered his
studio. The portraits went away in their
turn, but the pictures, after brief absences
at exhibitions, remained his own property,
testifying to the practical worthlessness of
the encouragement of his comrades, who

would sniff at his portraits of ladies and gentlemen, and prostrate themselves before his studies of gutter-snipe. It must be understood that no one of his artistic clique disapproved of his painting society portraits, for they had all adopted some means of gaining a livelihood outside of the special line of art which they, in their mistaken zeal, believed to be the only true and worthy one. Most of his comrades taught in the art schools of the city; some of the more fortunate ones conducted highly profitable private classes, where, at an enormously extravagant price per season, they actively stimulated and encouraged the artistic illusions of wealthy young ladies, and helped them to acquire a superficial and dangerous facility, which, for a future mistress of a house, is the most useless accomplishment imaginable.

Seymour was of an energetic and enterprising turn of mind, and if it had not been for his unwavering devotion to his artistic creed, he would have speedily made a wide reputation for himself as a painter with an original and charming talent. But accident

of situation had exposed him to the conta-
gion of realism, and the fever which seized
him in Paris was now kept alive, in a milder
form to be sure, by association with the
young painters in New York, who had been
abroad the same time as himself. After two
seasons at home he found his studio too
small and inconvenient, and he turned a
stable in the spacious back yard of his father's house, on one of the cross streets near
Fifth Avenue, into a fine studio, with a side
and top light, and transported thither his
easels, his bric-à-brac, and the lares and
penates of his Bohemian quarters. The new
studio was entered by a *porte-cochère* at one
side of the house, and was therefore as isolated and private as if it stood in the centre
of an acre of ground.

Among the sitters who came to him in his
new studio was Miss Margaret Van Hoorn,
the only daughter of a well-known wealthy
man, who had a stalwart pride in his Knick-
erbocker origin, and boasted generations of
opulent Van Hoorns before him. Miss Van
Hoorn was not an ordinary society belle, but

an intelligent, capable, sensible girl, and a favorite no less for the charm of her personal character than for a distinguished type of face and figure, which would stimulate the ambition of the most worn and weary portrait-painter.

Here, then, was Seymour's golden opportunity. He recognized it, and began to make the most of it by starting to paint a portrait of the young lady in a party dress. It had hitherto been his custom to deny to his sitters the privilege of watching his work in its various stages, but he was unable to refuse Miss Van Hoorn's request that she might be permitted to see the portrait in progress. Her desire to watch his work was excusable, because she had already taken lessons in painting, and had some little knowledge of technique. After the first sitting was over she occupied the divan under the large window, and chatted cheerfully an hour or more, thus initiating an intimacy which grew rapidly as the sittings went on. The painter, as long as he had his palette on his thumb, looked upon his sitter as a sort of autom-

aton, watched the pure lines of her neck and
arms with no conscious feeling except that
of keen anxiety to reproduce their grace,
and studied the mobile turn of the lips and
the varying curve of the eyelids with a
single-minded desire to catch something of
their charm and fix it on the canvas.

But soon another element crept insensibly
into the relation between sitter and painter,
and long before it was recognized by either
of them, became a potent factor in the grow-
ing problem. Miss Van Hoorn first began
to question Seymour about his artistic creed,
then showed an interest in his early life, thus
encouraging the artist to talk about himself.
She grew bold in criticising his work, and
even modestly declared her disapproval of
the confusion of his studio, and occasionally
gave to the arrangement of the objects a few
of those skilful feminine touches which add
an indefinable charm to any interior. The
artist, in his turn, suggested books for her to
read, frequently joined her in the box at the
Metropolitan Opera-house, accompanied her
to picture exhibitions, and even advised her

as to the color and style of dress most suited
to her complexion and figure. They were
all the while under the protection of that
unwritten social law which grants a certain
brief license to sitter and painter, which, like
the freedom of a picnic or an excursion
party, usually lasts no longer than the conditions which make this freedom innocent
and desirable.

"Mr. Seymour," said the sitter one day,
"why don't you paint an ideal subject, something classical or poetical?"

"I'm a realist, Miss Van Hoorn, and I
have come to the conclusion, since I began
your portrait, that I had better stick to copper pots and cabbages."

"But no one cares for copper pots and
cabbages, even if the former do have the
sheen of burnished gold, and the latter
sparkle with dew-drop jewels. I think every
painter ought to paint something more than
the surface of things."

"How about Vollon and—"

"You know," she interrupted, "I am not
far enough along, as you call it, to appreciate

the wild combinations of color and the
hodge-podge of splashes and dashes affected
by the modern school. I have tried to acquire this taste under your tuition, but I
cannot do it. I shall always believe in the
verdict of past centuries, that good art has
its reason in the immortalization of the beautiful."

" But there's Terburg—" he began.

" Raphael," she interrupted.

" Van der Meer de Delft," he suggested.

" Botticelli," she argued, and so the conversation went on, and at last ended, as discussions on religion, politics, and art always
do, in each declaring unwavering adherence
to original views.

Excursions to the art galleries and to the
Metropolitan Museum were often the result
of these little flutters; but although neither
the artist nor the sitter would confess to the
least disturbance of artistic faith, Seymour
actually began, before he knew why, to
select an ideal subject. Several motives
from classical poetry, from mythology, and
from modern writers came to his mind, and

he was unable to decide, nor did he know that he really cared to fix on any one of them. Meanwhile the sittings continued, and the portrait approached completion. Suddenly one day a compromise suggested itself to the painter, how or why he never knew, and he quietly remarked, " Miss Van Hoorn, I am going to paint a Medusa's head."

" Horrid," she said, frankly. " I hate snakes."

Seymour was somewhat discouraged by her impulsive disapproval of his subject, but, nevertheless, warmly defended his choice, and was all the more eloquent, perhaps, because he felt that she had recognized his ingenious compromise between idealism and realism. He insisted that the proportions of her face had suggested the subject to him, and was so serious in his assertion that she was in this degree responsible for his choice of motive, that she finally yielded to his eager solicitation, and consented to sit for the eyes and mouth of the Medusa's head.

The same afternoon he went down-town

to a shop near the docks, where all kinds of birds, animals, and reptiles were sold alive— a sort of depot, in fact, for the dime museums and small menageries — and bought a box of a dozen moccasin snakes recently arrived from the South. He selected this variety on account of the venomous appearance of the small heads, the repulsive thickness of the bodies, and the richness of color of the mottled scales, intending to make a close study of all the characteristics of this variety of the serpent. He could in this way heighten the contrast which he proposed to make between the calm beauty of the woman's face and the repulsiveness of the serpent locks. He ordered the box to be sent to his studio the same afternoon, and spent that evening in blocking out on the canvas a charcoal sketch of the head he had in his mind.

The following day was Sunday, and during the night a severe cold wave, accompanied by a blizzard of unusual severity, began to sweep over the city. Early on Monday morning the artist went around

into the studio, and was surprised to find
that the snow had blown in through the
ventilator, and that the temperature was
very low, notwithstanding the fact that a
fire had been kept up all the time in the
great magazine stove.   His first thought was
for the snakes, and, by no means certain that
they were not already frozen, he moved the
box near the fire, closed the ventilators in
the roof of the studio, opened the dampers
in the stove, and shook the grate, so as to
start the fire more briskly.

It was the last day Miss Van Hoorn could
come, because she was about to accompany
her family to Florida for a few weeks, and
in order to sit a little for the picture she had
promised to come earlier than usual.

Seymour, like all who were not obliged to
brave the blizzard on that now memorable
Monday, had no idea of the severity of the
storm which was raging, and was not surprised, therefore, at the appearance of his
sitter shortly after nine o'clock.   She was
accompanied, as usual, by her maid and by
her pug-dog.   Miss Van Hoorn never looked

more charming than she did at that moment,
for her cheeks were ruddy with the cold, and
her eyes sparkled with the excitement of
the drive.

"Do you know," she said, "we came very
near not getting here. The drifts were so
high that John was scarcely able to get the
horses through the street; and as for the
cold, I never felt anything like it. There
now, I do believe I have left my opera cloak
at home, and you must finish the drapery to-
day. You'll have to run back and bring it,"
she added, turning to her maid. "I don't
think the storm is as bad as it was; the wind
does not sound so loud, at any rate."

The maid courageously set out on her
walk, but before she crossed the avenue was
blown down, half smothered with the snow
and half frozen, and was finally rescued by a
policeman, who carried her into the base-
ment of the nearest house, where she was
obliged to remain the larger part of the day.

Meanwhile the artist and his sitter sat for
a long time beside the fire, expecting the return of the maid at every moment. Almost

the first thing Miss Van Hoorn noticed was the box of snakes, and, although she was horrified and disgusted at the first sight of them, soon began to look at them with interest, because the artist was so enthusiastic about the use he proposed to make of them, and so full of the picture he had begun. The glass in front of the box was slightly clouded by vapor condensed by the change in temperature, and in order to examine more closely the beautiful colors of the scales, Seymour took out the glass, placed it on top of the box, and went to get a paint-rag to wipe off the vapor. The moccasins made no sign of life.

Miss Van Hoorn was very much interested in the charcoal sketch of the head, criticised it frankly and freely, and they both grew quite absorbed in the changes the artist rapidly made in the proportions of the face. The loud striking of the antique clock soon reminded them, however, that the hour for the sitting was long past, and that the portrait was of more present importance than the embryonic picture.

12

The artist was shortly busy with his painting, and the sitter, now well accustomed to the pose, endeavored to facilitate the progress of the work by remaining as quiet as possible. The silence of the studio was broken only by the stertorous breathing of the pug, asleep on the Turkish carpet in front of the stove, and by the rattle of the sleet against the large window.

Suddenly the shrill yelps of the dog startled them from their preoccupation. On the carpet, near the stove, one of the moccasins was coiled, ready to strike the pug, who, in an agony of terror, could not move a foot, but only uttered wild and piercing shrieks.

"Never mind; I'll soon settle him," said Seymour; and he rushed at the snake with his maul-stick. But before he could cross the room, the moccasin had struck his victim; and as the artist shattered his slender stick at the first blow, he saw that the box was empty, and that the other snakes were wriggling around the studio.

Miss Van Hoorn was transfixed with

horror, but she neither shrieked nor fainted, although she looked as if she would
swoon before Seymour could reach her.
The pair were fairly surrounded by the
reptiles before the artist had time to think
of another weapon.

The only thing to do in the emergency
occurred to both of them at the same instant, and in a much shorter time than
it takes to tell it Miss Van Hoorn was
safely perched on the solid crossbar of the
French easel, four feet or more from the
ground; and the painter, who had hastily
thrown the portrait on the floor, face up-
ward, was standing on the shelf.

Knowing the venomous character of the
moccasin, Seymour was not eager for a
fight with the snakes, particularly since he
was without a weapon. It was impossible
to reach the trophy of Turkish yataghans
on the farther wall of the studio without
encountering at least two of the reptiles,
and after a moment's consideration he
climbed up and sat down beside Miss Van
Hoorn, *tête-à-tête* fashion, and, like herself,

put his arm around the upright piece between them.

Neither one of them spoke for a moment;
and then he, overcome with remorse at his
carelessness, and trembling at the possible
result of the adventure, exclaimed, in a tone
of despair, " Here's a situation !"

This commonplace remark did not carry
with it a hint of a satisfactory solution of
the difficulty, and he felt this the moment
he had uttered it. Miss Van Hoorn made
no reply, but with pale cheeks and frightened eyes sat silent, clinging almost convul-
sively to her support.

"We can easily bring the people by
shouting," suggested her companion.

"No, no!" she half gasped. "What a
ridiculous position to be found in! Indeed,
I—I— Are you sure the neighbors cannot see through the window?"

"Of course they can't; it's corrugated
glass. But then, after all, if any one should
come, the moccasins might bite them, and
we should be no better off."

The snakes became more and more active.

"MISS VAN HOORN WAS SAFELY PERCHED ON THE SOLID
CROSSBAR."

The pug lay in his last death-agonies, and as he struggled on the carpet, almost under their feet, the soft fingers of the young lady instinctively found their way to the firm, muscular hand of the artist, and closed around it with a confiding pressure, as if she recognized in him her sole protector in this danger, and had great need of his sympathy and support.

If the truth must be told, her sweet unconsciousness was not shared by her companion, for he felt a distinct sense of satisfaction at the touch of her hand, and this sensation fully dominated for a moment the complex feeling of relief at escape from recent imminent danger and of great present perplexity, uncertainty, and fear.

They were now fairly besieged; and although no harm could come to them in their present position, it was by no means comfortable to sit perched on a narrow oak bar, and it was impossible to tell how or when they would be delivered from their enemy.

A strange and oppressive silence seemed to have come over the whole city; not so much a silence, perhaps, as an unusual muffling of all the ordinary sounds of traffic and activity. The swish of the sleet against the window was almost continuous, but when it ceased for a moment there was heard no rattle of the streets, no rumble of the horse-cars, no clatter of trains on the elevated railroad. Instead of these familiar sounds, a wide, deep, and ominous murmur filled the air. This was not a loud and heavy sound, like the roar of the ocean, nor yet shrill, like the rush and whistling of a gale, but had a peculiar low and muffled quality that made a weird accompaniment to the dramatic situation of the artist and sitter in the storm-and-serpent-beleaguered studio.

There was a horrible fascination in watching the movements of the snakes as they restlessly glided from one part of the studio to another, the scales on their thick repulsive bodies glistening. in the strong light, and flashing a variety of colors. The stove was now red-hot, and the fire was roaring loudly. In spite of the intense cold outside, the heat became oppressive at the height where they sat, and Miss Van Hoorn, whose nerves were much shaken by her fright, and kept in a flutter by the movements of the snakes below, began to feel faint. The house-servants had standing orders never to interrupt the sittings on any excuse until the artist rang for luncheon. It was now half-past eleven, and Seymour, despairing of the return of the maid, at last resolved to shout as loudly as possible, and to stop the servant from opening the door by calling out to him as he came along the passageway. He explained this plan to Miss Van Hoorn, and proceeded to shout and halloo with the full strength of his lungs. He waited a few moments, but no sound of footsteps was heard, and then he shouted again and again. Still the roaring of the fire, the grumble of the storm, and the hideous rustling of the snakes alone greeted their eager ears. At last he was obliged to conclude that the noise of the storm prevented his cries from reaching the house.

What to do next he did not know, but as he was fanning Miss Van Hoorn with a letter out of his pocket—indeed, with one of her own notes to him—he struck upon a plan of letting in air, and at the same time attracting the attention of some one. When the brief faint turn had passed off, he climbed down to the shelf, gathered up his tubes of color, and returned to his perch. After a few vigorous throws with the heaviest tubes, he succeeded in breaking one of the panes of the large window, and a fierce gust of wind blew upon them. To their great disappointment the opening in the glass disclosed only the blank wall of the opposite extension; and as he had wasted all his heavy ammunition, he could not break another pane higher up in the window. He tried shouting again, but with no result.

The situation was now worse than before, for Miss Van Hoorn was in her even-

ing dress and exposed to the freezing
draught of a blizzard. Seymour persuaded her to put on his velveteen jacket, and,
after a few attempts, succeeded in tearing
down a curtain that hung from the ceiling alongside the opening in the roof in
order to cast a shadow on the background.
This he wrapped around both of them,
then sat and considered what to do next.
No new plan, however, suggested itself
to either of them. They did not talk
much, for they were too seriously occupied with the problem of escape to waste
words. The single hand of the antique
clock moved with agonizing slowness, and
the pair sat there a long time in silence,
shivering, despairing. Once or twice a
sense of the ludicrousness of their position came over them, and they laughed a
little; but their mirth was almost hysterical, and was succeeded by a greater de-
pression of spirits than before. Seymour
had proposed several times to make a dash
for the door, but two or three of the reptiles were always moving about between

the easel and the entrance, and Miss Van Hoorn entreated him tearfully not to attempt it. The cold seemed to increase, and Seymour soon noticed that the fire was burning itself out. This was a new source of anxiety, and neither of them cared to anticipate their sufferings on the top of the easel with the temperature below zero.

"Just look at the snakes!" suddenly cried Seymour, in great excitement.

Miss Van Hoorn was startled by the vehemence of his cry, and could only gasp: "No, no! I can't bear to look at them any more."

"The cold is making them torpid again," he fairly shrieked, in the joy of his discovery. "How stupid not to have thought of this before!" he added, in a tone of disgust.

He was right. One by one they ceased to crawl, and those nearest the window soon lay motionless. Checking his impatience to descend on the snakes until those by the stove ceased to show signs of active life, he dropped from the perch, seized a yataghan from the wall, and speedily despatched them all.

Miss Van Hoorn anxiously watched the slaughter from the safe elevation of the easel, and, when it was over, fainted into the artist's arms.

The most unique and remarkable en-gagement ring ever marked with a date at Tiffany's was a beautiful antique in-taglio of Medusa's head set in Etruscan gold.

THE FOURTH WAITS

THE FOURTH WATCH

THE FOURTH WAITS

I.

THE click of dominos is an accompaniment scarcely in harmony with a discussion of psychology and religion. But no
subject is too sacred, or too profane, to be
discussed in a café—that neutral ground
where all parties and all sects meet; and it
was a serious debate during a game of dominos that marked the beginning of a course
of strange coincidences and sad occurrences
that crowd one chapter in an eventful Bohemian life.

There were four of us art-students in the
Academy of Antwerp assembled, as was our
custom after the evening life-class, at a café
in a quiet *faubourg* of the city. It was a
gloomy November evening, cold and raw in
the wind, but not too chill to sit in the open

air under the lee of the wooden shed which enclosed two sides of the café garden. The heavy atmosphere had not crushed every spark of cheerfulness out of the buoyant natures of the materialistic Flemings, and the tables were filled with noisy *bourgeois* and their families, drinking the mild beer of Louvain or generous cups of coffee. Their gayety seemed sacrilegious in the solemn presence of approaching winter—that long, depressing, ghostly season which in the Low Countries gives warning of its coming with prophetic sobs and continued tears, and trails the shroud of summer before the eyes of shrinking mortals for weeks before it buries its victim. In a climate like that of Flanders, the winter, rarely marked by severe cold, really begins with the rainy season in early autumn, and it continues in an interminable succession of dismal days with shrouded skies.

On the evening in question the clouds seemed lower than usual; the wind was fitful and spasmodic, and came in long, mournful, insinuating sighs that stole in

mockingly between the peals of music and
laughter, and startled every one in his gay-
est mood.   The gas-jets flickered and
wavered weirdly, and the dry leaves danced
accompaniment to the movements of the
swift-footed waiters.   The clatter of wooden
shoes on the pavement without, and the
measureless but not unmusical songs of the
jolly workmen on their way home, filled the
score of the medley of sounds that broke
the sepulchral quiet of the evening.

There were four of us, as I have said: old
Reiner, Tyck, Henley, and myself.   Each
represented a different nationality.   Reiner
was a Norwegian of German descent, tall and
ungainly, with a large head, a shock of light-
colored, coarse hair, a virgin beard, and a
good-humored face focused in a pair of
searching gray eyes that pried their way into
everything that came under their owner's observation.   He was by no means a handsome
man, neither was he unattractive; and his
sober habits, cool judgment, and great stock
of general information gained for him the
familiar name of old Reiner among the more

13

thoughtless and more superficial students
who were his friends. He was by nature of
a more scientific than artistic turn of mind.
He was conversant with nine languages, in-
cluding Sanskrit, had received a thorough
university education in Norway and Germany, took delight in investigating every
subject that came in his way—from the habits of an ant to the movements of the gold
market in America—and could talk intelli-
gently and instructively on every topic proposed to him. Indeed, his scientific and lit-
erary attainments were a wonder to the rest
of us, who had lived quite as long and had
accomplished much less. As an artist he had
great talents as well ; but here also his love
of investigation constantly directed his efforts. In his academic course he had less
success than might have been anticipated,
except in the direction of positive rendering
of certain effects. He was not a colorist ;
such natures rarely are ; and it is probable
that he would never have made a brilliant
artist in any branch of the profession, for he
was too much of a positivist, and even his

historical pictures would have been little
more than marvels of correctness of costume
and accessories.   In his association with us,
the flow of his abundant good-humor, which
sometimes seemed unlimited, was interrupted
by occasional spells of complete reaction,
when he neither spoke to nor even saw any
one else, but made a hermit of himself until
the mood had passed.

Tyck at first sight looked like a Spaniard.
He was slight in stature, one short leg causing a stoop which made him appear still
smaller than he was. His skin was of a clear
brown, warmed by an abundance of rich
blood ; a mass of strong, curling hair, and a
black moustache and imperial framed in a
face of peculiar strong beauty. His eyes had
something in them too deep to be altogether
pleasing, for they caused one to look at him
seriously, yet they were as full of laughter
and good-nature and cheerfulness as dark
eyes can be.   His face was one that, notwithstanding its peculiarities, gave a good
first impression ; and a long friendship had
proved him to be chargeable with fewer

blemishes of character than are written down
against the most of us.   But his hands were
not in his favor.   They were long, bony, and
cold ; the finger-joints were large and lacked
firmness, and the pressure of the hand was
listless or unsympathetic.   The lines of life
were faint and discouraging, and there were
few prominent marks in the palm.   The secret of his complexion lay in his parentage,
for his mother was a native woman of Java,
and his father a Dutch merchant, who settled
in that far-off country, built up a fortune, and
raised a small family of boys, who deserted
the paternal nest as soon as they were old
enough to flutter alone.   Tyck was a colorist.   He seemed to see the tones of nature
rich with the warm reflections of a tropical
sun; and his studies from life, while strong
and luscious in tone, were full of fire and subtle gradations — qualities combined rarely
enough in the works of older artists.   He
was to all appearance in the flush of health,
and, notwithstanding his deformity, was uncommonly active and fond of exercise.   We
who knew him intimately, however, always

looked upon him as a marked man. With
all his rugged, healthy look, his physique was
not vigorous enough to resist the attacks of
the common foe, winter, and we knew that
he occasionally pined mentally and physi-
cally for the luxurious warmth of his native
land. He flourished in the raw climate of
Flanders only as a transplanted flower flour-
ishes; still, he was not declining in health or
strength.

It is a long and delicate process to build
up an intimate friendship between men of
mercurial temperament and such an imper-
sonation of coolness and deliberation and
studied manners as was Henley, the third
member of our group. From his type of
face and his peculiar bearing he was easily
recognizable as an Englishman, and even as
a member of the Church of England. His
manner was plainly the result of a severe
and formal training; his whole life, as he told
us himself, had been passed under the careful surveillance of a strict father, who was for
a long time the rector of one of the first
churches of London. But Henley, serious,

formal, and cool, was not uncompanionable; and I am not quite sure whether it was not the bony thinness of his face, his straggling black beard and abundant dead-colored hair, that predisposed one at first sight to judge him as a sort of melancholy black sheep among his lighter-hearted companions. So we all placed him at our first meeting. When once the ice was broken, and we felt the sympathetic presence that surrounded him in his intercourse with friends, he became a necessity to complete the current of our little circle, and his English steadiness often served a good purpose in many wordy tempests.

In religious opinions we four were as divided as we were distinct in nationality. Henley, as I have said, was a member of the Church of England. Tyck was a Jew and a Freemason. Reiner entirely disbelieved in everything that was not plain to him intellectually. Our discussions on religious subjects were long and warm, for the theories of the fourth member of the circle piled new fuel upon the flames that sprang up under the friction of the ideas of the other three, and on these topics alone we were seriously at variance. Rarely were our disputes carried to that point where either of us felt wounded after the discussion was ended, but on more than one occasion they were violent enough to have ruptured our little bond if it had not been strengthened by ties of more than ordinary friendship.

This friendship was of the unselfish order, too. We were in the habit of living on the share-and-share-alike principle. Henley was the only one who had any allowance, and he always felt that his regular remittance was rather a bar to his complete and unqualified admission to our little ring. The joint capital among us was always kept in circulation. When one had money and the others had none, and it suited our inclinations or the purposes of our study to visit the Dutch cities, or even to cross the Channel, we travelled on the common purse. Share-and-share-alike in cases less pressing than sickness or actual want may not be a sound mercantile principle; but where the freemasonry of mutual tastes, united purposes, and com-

mon hardships binds friend to friend, the
spirit of communism is half the charm of existence. Especially is this true of Bohemian
life.

In introducing the characters a little time
has been taken, partly in order to give us a
chance to move our table into a more shel-
tered corner, and to allow us to get well
started in another game of dominos. As I
remember that evening, Reiner, who had not
entirely recovered from an attack of one of
his peculiar moods, had been discussing mira-
cles and mysteries with more than his accustomed warmth, and the rest of us had been
cornered and driven off the field in turn;
even to Henley, who was not, with all his
study, quite as well up on the subject of the
Jewish priests and the Druids as old Reiner,
whom no topic seemed to find unprepared.
When the discussion was at its height I observed in Reiner certain uneasy movements,
and I instinctively looked behind him to see
if any one was watching him, as his actions
resembled those of a person under the mes-
merism of an unseen eye. I saw no one, and

concluded that my imagination had deceived
me. But Reiner became suddenly grave and
even solemn, and the debate stopped entirely. At last, after a long silence, Reiner
proposed another game of dominos. When
the pieces were distributed he began the
moves, saying at the same time, quite in
earnest and as if talking to himself, "This
will decide it."

His voice was so strange and his look so
determined that we felt that something was
at stake, and instinctively and in chorus declared that it was useless to play the game
out, and proposed an adjournment to the
sketching-club. Reiner did not object, and
we rose to go. As we left the table I saw
behind Reiner's chair two small, luminous,
green balls, set in a black mass, turned towards us—evidently the eyes of a dog, glistening in the reflection of the gas like emerald
fires. Possibly the others did not notice the
animal, and I was too much startled at the
discovery of the unseen eye to speak of it at
that moment. Before I had recovered myself completely we were out of the gate, fol-

lowed by the dog. Under the street-lamp, he leaped about and seemed quite at home. He was seen to be a perfectly black Spitz poodle, with cropped ears and tail, very lively in his movements, and with a remarkably intelligent expression. He was a dog of a character not commonly met, and once observed was not easily mistaken for others of the same breed. Our walk to the club was dreary enough. The gloomy manner of old Reiner was contagious, and no one spoke a word. I was too busy reflecting on the strange manner in which our game had been interrupted to occupy myself with my companion, remembering the now frequent recurrence of Reiner's blue days, and dreading his absence from the class and the club, which I knew from experience was sure to follow such symptoms as I had observed in the café. To the sketching-club we brought an atmosphere so forbidding that it seemed as if we were the heralds of some misfortune. Scarcely a cheerful word was said after our entrance, and frequent glasses of Louvain or *d'orge*, drunk on the production of new cari-

catures, failed to raise the barometer of our
spirits. The meeting broke up early, and we
four separated. The dog, which had been
lying under a settee near the door, followed
Reiner as he turned down the boulevard.

For a week we did not meet again. Reiner
kept his room or was out of town. He made
no sign, and without him we frequented
neither the café nor the club. The weather
grew cold and rainy ; the last evening at the
café proved to have been the final gasp of
dying autumn, and winter had fairly begun.
At last Reiner made his appearance at dinner one dark afternoon, and took his accustomed seat at our table, near the window
which opened out upon the glass-covered
court-yard of the small hotel where we used
to dine, a score of us, artists and students
all. He looked very weary and hollow-eyed;
said he had been unwell, had taken an over-
dose of laudanum for neuralgia, and had
been confined to his room for a few days.
Expecting each day to be able to go out the
next morning, he had neglected to send us
word, and so the week had passed. As he

was speaking I noticed a dog in the court-
yard, the same black poodle that attached
himself to us in the café. Reiner, observing
my surprise, explained that the dog had been
living with him at his room in the Steen-
houwersvest, and that they were inseparable
companions now. We could all see that old
Reiner was not yet himself again. One of
us ventured to suggest that there might be
something Mephistophelian about the animal, and that Reiner was endeavoring, Faust-
like, to get at the kernel of the beast, so as
to fathom whatever mystery of heaven or
earth was as yet to him inexplicable. No
further remarks were made, as Reiner arose
to go away, leaving his dinner untouched.
He shook hands with us all almost solemnly, and with the poodle went out into the
gloomy street.

Another week passed, and we saw neither
Reiner nor the poodle. December began,
and the days were short and dark, the sun
scarcely appearing above the cathedral roof
in his course from east to west. The absence of old Reiner was a constant theme of

conversation, and there were multitudes of conjectures as to whether he were in love, in debt, or really ill. We had no message from him, not a word, not a written line.

One evening as we sat at dinner—it was Thursday, and a heavy rain was falling—the black poodle dashed suddenly in, closely followed by Reiner's servant-girl, bonnetless and in slippers, and drenched to the skin. Her message was guessed before she had time to gasp out, "Och, Mynheeren, uwer vriend Reiner is dood!" Not waiting for explanations, we followed her as she returned through the slippery streets, scarcely walking or running. How I got there I never knew; it seemed at the time as if I were carried along by some superior force. Filled with dread and fear, mingled with hope that it was an awful mistake and that something might yet be done, I reached the door of the house. Through the grocery-shop, where was assembled a crowd of shivering, drenched people who had gathered there on hearing of the event, conscious that all were watching our entrance with solemn sympathy, not seeing distinctly any one or anything, forgetting the narrow, dark, and winding wooden stair, I was at the door of Reiner's room in an instant. The tall figure of a gendarme was silhouetted against the window; a few women stood by the table whispering together, awe-stricken at the sight of something that was before them, to the left, and still hidden from me as I took in the scene on entering the door.

Another step brought me to the bedside. There in the dim light lay old Reiner, not as if asleep, for the awful pallor of death was on his face, but with an expression as calm and peaceful as if he were soon to awake from pleasant dreams, as if his soul were still dreaming on. He lay on his right side, with his head resting on his doubled arm. The bedclothes were scarcely disturbed, and his left arm lay naturally on the sheet which was turned over the coverlid. Great, dark stains splashed the wall behind the bed and the pillow; dark streaks ran along over the linen and made little pools upon the floor. His shirt-bosom was one broad, irregular blotch

of blood, and in his left hand I could see the
carved ivory handle of the little Scandinavian
sheath-knife that he always carried in his
belt. Before I had fully comprehended the
awful reality of poor Reiner's death, the doctor arrived, lights were brought, and the examination began. Our dead comrade's head
being raised and his shirt-bosom opened,
there were exposed two great gashes across
the left jugular vein and one across the right,
and nine deep wounds in the breast. Few
of the cuts would not have proved mortal,
and the ferocity with which the fatal knife
had been plunged again and again into his
breast testified to the madness of the de-
termination to destroy his life. On the dress-
ing-table by the bed we found two small
laudanum vials, both empty, and one over-
turned, as if placed hastily beside its fellow.
In all probability poor Reiner took this large
dose of laudanum early in the morning, as it
was found that he had been in bed during
the entire day, and was seen by the servant
to be sleeping at three o'clock in the afternoon. His iron constitution and great phys-

ical strength overcoming the effects of the narcotic, he probably awoke to consciousness late in the afternoon. Finding himself still alive, in the agonies of despair and disappointment at the unsuccessful attempt to dream over the chasm into the next world, he seized his knife and madly stabbed himself, doubtless feeling little pain, and only happily conscious that his long-planned step was successfully taken at last. The room was unchanged, nothing was disturbed, and there was no evidence of the premeditation of the suicide, except an open letter on the table, addressed to us, his friends. It contained a simple statement of his reasons for leaving the world, saying that he was discouraged with his progress in art, that he could not establish himself as an artist without great expense to his family and friends, and that he believed by committing suicide he simply annihilated himself—nothing more or less— and so ceased to trouble himself or those interested in him. He gave no directions as to the disposal of his effects, but enclosed a written confession of faith, which read:

" Frederik Reiner, athée, ne croyant à rien que ce que l'on peut prouver par la raison et l'expérience. Croyant tout de même à l'existence d'un esprit, mais d'un esprit qui dissoud et disparaît avec le corps.

" L'âme c'est la vie, c'est un complexité des forces qui sont inséparables des atoms ou des molecules dont se compose le corps. L'un comme l'autre a existé depuis l'éternité. Moi-même, mon âme comme mon corps, un complexité accidentel, une réunion passagère.

" J'insisterai toujours dans les éléments qui me composent mais dissoudent en d'autres complexités. Ainsi, *moi, ma personnalité*, n'existera plus après ma mort."

Beside this letter on the table lay Henri Murger's "Scènes de la Vie de Bohème," open, face downward. The pages contained the description of the death of one of the artists, and the following brief and touching sentence was underlined : " *Il fut enterré quelquepart.*" A litter was brought from the hospital, and four men carried away the body ; the dog, which we had come to look

14

upon almost with horror, closely following the melancholy procession as it gradually disappeared in the drizzling gloom of the narrow streets. We three went to our rooms in a strange bewilderment, and huddled together in speechless grief and horror around the little fireplace. When bedtime came we separated and tried to sleep, but I doubt if an eye was closed or the awful vision of poor Reiner, as we last saw him, left either of us for a moment.

The days that followed were, to me at least, most agonizing. The terrible death of old Reiner grew less and less repulsive and more horribly absorbing. I had often read of the influence of such examples on peculiarly constituted minds, but had never before felt the dread and ghastly fascination which seemed to grow upon me as the days following the tragedy drew no veil across the awful spectacle, ever present in my mind's eye, but rather added vividness and distinctness to the smallest details of the scene. My bed, with its white curtains, the conventional pattern of heavy Flemish furniture found in every room, came to be almost a tomb, in the morbid state of my imagination. I could never look at its long, spotless drapery without fancying my own head on the pillow, my own blood on the wall and staining with splashes of deep red the curtain and sheets. The number and shape of the spots on old Reiner's bed seemed photographed on the retina of my eye, and danced upon the slender, graceful folds of the curtains as often as I dared look at them. A little nickel-plated derringer, always lying on my table as a paper-weight, often found its way into my hands, and I would surprise myself wondering whether death by such a means were not, after all, preferable to destruction by the knife. A few cartridges in the corner of my closet, which I had hidden away to keep them from the meddling hands of the servant, seemed to draw me towards them with a constant magnetism. I could not forget that shelf and that particular spot behind a bundle of paint-rags. If there was need of anything on that particular shelf for months after Reiner's death, I always took it quickly and resolutely, shutting the closet door as if I were shutting in all the evil spirits that could possess me. The tempter was exorcised, but with difficulty, and to this day, for all I know, the cartridges may still lie hidden there. Then, too, a quaint Normandy hunting-knife was quite as fiendish in its influence as the derringer. Its ugly, crooked blade, and strong, sharp point were very suggestive, and for a time I was almost afraid to touch the handle, lest the demon of suicide should overcome me. Still, in the climax of this fever, which might well have resulted in the suicide of another of the four, for it was evident that Henley and Tyck were also under the same influences that surrounded me day and night, the thought of burdening our friends with our dead bodies was the strongest inducement that stayed our hands. It is certain that if we had been situated where the disposal of our bodies would have been a matter of little or no difficulty—as, for example, on board ship—one or perhaps all three of us would have succumbed to the influence of the mania that possessed us.

It was on the Sunday forenoon—a grim, gray morning threatening a storm—following the fatal Thursday, that we met in the court-yard of the city hospital to bury poor Reiner.

The hideous barrenness of a Flemish burial-ground, even in bright, cheerful weather, is enough to crush the most buoyant spirits; it is indescribably oppressive and soul-sickening. The awful desolation of the place in the dreariness of that day will ever remain a horrid souvenir in my mind. Nature did not seem to weep, but to frown; and in the heavy air one felt a deep and solemn reproach. The soaked and dull atmosphere was stifling in its density, like the overloaded breath from some newly opened tomb. There was an army of felt but unseen spirits lurking in the ghostly quiet of the place, which the presence of a hundred mortals did not disturb. There was no breath of wind, and the settling of the snow and a faint, faint moan of the distant rushing tide made the silence more oppressive. The drip of the water from the drenched mosses on the brick walls; the faintest rustle of the wreaths of immortelles hung on every hideous black cross; the fall of one withered flower from the forgotten offerings of some friend of the buried dead—every sound at other times and in other places quite inaudible, broke upon that unearthly quiet with startling distinctness. The sound of our footsteps, as we followed the winding path to the fresh heap of earth in a remote corner, fell heavily on the thick air, and the high brick walls, mouldy and rotting in the sunless angles, gave a deep and unwilling echo. It was like treading the dark and skull-walled passages of the Catacombs without the grateful veil of a partial darkness. All that was mortal and subject to decay, all that was to our poor human understanding immortal and indestructible, seemed buried alike in this rigid, barren enclosure. Beyond? There was no beyond; the straight, barren walls on all sides, and the impenetrable murkiness of the gray vault that covered us, barred out the material and the spiritual world. Here was the end, here all was certain and defined

—a narrow ditch, a few shovelfuls of earth, and nothing more that needed or invited explanation. There was no future, no waking from that sleep: all exit from that narrow and pitiless graveyard seemed forever closed. Such thoughts as these were, until then, strangers to us. Could it be the unextinguishable influence of that nerveless body that filled the place with the dread and uncongenial presence that urged us to accept for the time, then and there, the theories and convictions of the mind which once animated that cold and motionless mass?

The fresh, moist earth was piled on one side of the grave, and the workmen with their shovels stood near the heap as we filed up, and at a sign lowered the coffin into the grave. A Norwegian minister approached to conduct the services. He took his place apart from all, at the head of the grave, and began with the customary prayer in the Norwegian language. He was dressed in harmony with the day and scene. A long, black gown fell to the feet and was joined by a

single row of thickly sewn buttons; a white
band hung from his neck low down in front,
and white wristbands half covered his gloved
hands; a silk hat completed the costume.
His face was of the peculiar, emotionless
Northern type, perfectly regular in feature,
with well-trimmed reddish-brown beard and
hair, and small, unsympathetic gray eyes,
and it bore an expression of congealed conviction in the severity of divine judgment.
His prayer was long and earnest, and the
discourse which followed was full of honest
regret for the loss of our friend, but mainly
charged with severe reproach against the
wickedness of the suicide, the burden of the
sermon being, "The wages of sin is death."
We stood there, shivering with the pene-
trating chill of the damp atmosphere, filled
with the horrors of this acre of the dead, and
listened patiently to the long discourse.   In
the very middle of the argument there was
a sudden rustle near the head of the grave,
a momentary confusion among those standing near the minister, and, to the great
amazement and horror of Tyck, Henley, and

myself, that black poodle, draggled but dig-
nified, walked quietly to the edge of the pit
as if he had been bidden to the funeral, and
sat down there, midway between the minister
and the little knot of mourners, eying first
the living and then the dead with calm and
portentous gravity. He seemed to pay the
closest attention to the words of the discourse, and with an expression of intelligent
triumph, rather than grief, cocked his wise
little head to one side and eyed the minister
as he dilated on the sin of suicide, and then
looked solemnly down into the grave. His
actions were so human and his expression
so fiendishly exultant that to the three of us,
who had previously made his acquaintance,
his presence was an additional horror; among
the rest it merely excited comment on the
sagacity of the beast. There he sat through
the whole of the services, and nothing could
move him from his post.

At the close of the sermon, and after a
short eulogy in Flemish delivered by one
of us, the minister gave out the Norwegian
hymn with this refrain:

" Min Gud! gjör dog for Christi Blod
Min sidste Afskedstime god!"

The first part of the air is weird and Northern,
and the last strain is familiar to us by the
name of " Hebron." The Norwegian words
were significant and well-chosen for this occasion, very like the simple stanzas of our
" Hebron." The hymn is sad enough at all
times ; when tuned to the mournful drag of
our untrained voices it seemed like the sigh-
ing of unshrived spirits.

As the sad measures wailed forth, the day
seemed to grow colder and darker ; a dreary
wind rustled the dry branches of the stunted
trees, and rattled the yellow wreaths of immortelles and the dry garlands and bouquets.
The dog grew uneasy between the verses,
and howled long and piteously, startling us
all in our grief, and causing a dismal echo
from the cold, bare walls that hemmed us
in. At last the painfully long hymn was
ended, immortelles were placed upon the
coffin-lid, each one threw in a handful of
earth, and we turned our faces towards the
gate, away from death and desolation to

dismal and melancholy life and our now distasteful occupation. With one last look into the enclosure, we passed out of the gate, closing it behind us. The dog was still at his post.

A rapid drive brought us in fifteen minutes to the Place de Meir, where we alighted and found to welcome us the same black poodle that we left at the grave. The cemetery of Kiel is at least two miles from the Place de Meir; yet the dog left it after we did, and, panting and covered with mud, was awaiting us at the latter place. He could have made his escape from the cemetery only by the aid of some one to open the heavy gate for him, and, considering this necessary delay, his appearance in the city before us was, to say the least, startling. He welcomed us cheerfully, but we gave him no encouragement. The inexplicable ubiquity of the beast horrified us too much to allow any desire for such a companion. As we separated and took three different roads, to my great relief he followed neither of us, but stood undecided which way to turn.

The circumstances attending the burial of poor Reiner and the events which followed tended to increase our disposition to imitate the questionable action of our friend; but the annual *concours* of the academy, which demanded the closest attention and the most severe work for nearly three months, counteracted all such evil tendencies, and by spring-time we laughed at the morbid fancies of the previous winter.

The evening after the funeral, on my way to the life class, I met the poodle again, and, in reply to his recognition, drove him away with my cane. Both Tyck and Henley related at the class a similar experience with the dog, which we had now come to look upon as a fiend in disguise. After this the meetings with the poodle were daily and almost hourly. He would quietly march into the hotel court-yard as we were at dinner; we would stumble over him on the stairs; at a café the *garçon* would hunt him from the room; at the academy he would startle us, amuse the rest of the students, and enrage the professor by breaking the guard of the old surveillant, and rushing into the life class. He seemed to belong to no one and to have no home, and yet he was an attractive animal with his long, glossy coat, saucy ears and tail, and bright, intelligent eyes. We often endeavored to rid ourselves of him. Many times I tried my best to kill him, arming myself expressly with my heavy stick; but he avoided all my attacks, and always met me cheerfully at our next interview. At times he was morose and meditative. It used to be a theory of mine that at these seasons he was making up his mind which one of us he had better adopt as his master, declaring—only half in earnest, however—that the one whom the animal especially favored would be sure to meet poor Reiner's fate. The months of January and February passed, and the poodle still haunted us. In the course of these dark months we repeatedly attempted to make friends with the dog, finding that we could not make an enemy of him, and hoped thus to disprove the imagined fatality of the beast or else to break the spell by our own wills. All efforts at conciliation failed; he would never enter even to take food the room where we three were alone, and would show signs of general recognition only, and those but sparingly, when we were together. He seemed content with simply watching us, and not desirous of further acquaintance. Yet, in the face of this mysterious behavior, I doubt very much if any one of us really believed that anything would come of our forebodings; for we began to speak of the dog at first quite in jest, and grew more serious only as we were impressed after the death of Reiner by the consistent impartiality of his fondness for our society, and by the unequalled persistency with which he haunted us wherever we went abroad.

We made inquiries about the dog at the house where old Reiner used to live, and diligently searched various localities, but we could not find out where he passed his nights, and we discovered only that he was known all about the town simply as Reiner's dog, the story of his presence at the funeral having been repeated by some of those who noticed his actions at the grave. March came and went, and the dog had not yet taken his choice of us, and we began to be confident that he never would. But in one of the first warm days of spring we noticed his absence, and for a day or two saw nothing of him. One Sunday, after a fête-day when we three had not met as usual at the academy, a pure spring day, I received a short note from Henley, asking me to come to his room on the Place Verte, as he was unwell. I went immediately to his lodgings, and found him sitting up, but quite pale and with a changed expression on his face. I knew he had been suffering from a severe cold for some time, but we all had colds in the damp, unhealthful old academy. His noticeably increasing paleness was due, I had supposed, to the anxious labor and prolonged strain of the *concours*. In one instance when we had been for thirty-six hours shut up in a room with sealed doors and windows, threescore of us, together with as many large kerosene lamps and nearly the same number of foul pipes, with three large, red-hot cylinder stoves, and no exit allowed on any excuse, we were all more or less affected by the poisoned air and the long struggle with the required production. The idea, then, that there was anything serious the matter with Henley never entered my head as I saw him sitting there in his room; but his first words brought me to a realization of the case, and all the horror of that long winter and its one mournful event came back to me in a flash. His remark was significant. He simply said, "That dog is here."

To be sure, the poodle was quietly sleeping near Henley's easel, in the sun. After a few general remarks, my friend said to me, quite abruptly, as if he had made up his mind to come to the point at once:

"I thought I would send for you, old boy, to give you a souvenir or two. I am more seriously ill than you imagine. My brother will be here to-morrow; I shall return with him to England, and you and I shall probably meet no more."

There was resignation in every word he uttered, and he was evidently convinced of

the hopelessness of attempting to struggle
with the disease, his languid efforts to throw
it off not having in the least retarded its advance.   I tried to prove to him the folly of
the superstition about the dog, but it was
useless.   He quietly said that the doctor had
assured him of the necessity of an immediate
return to a warmer climate and to the care
of his friends.   Tyck, who had been sent for
at the same time, came in shortly after, and
was completely shaken by the strange fulfilment of our mysterious forebodings.   We
passed a sad hour in that little room, and
took our leave only when we saw that Henley was fatigued with too much talking, for
he began to cough frightfully, and could hardly speak above a whisper.   He gave to each
of us, with touching tenderness, a palette-
knife—the best souvenirs we could have, he
said, because they would be in our hands constantly—and we took our leave, promising to
meet him on the boat the following day.   We
learned from the servant that the poodle had
inhabited the cellar for several days, and that
they had not been able to drive him away.

15

Tyck seemed perfectly dazed by the severity of Henley's malady and the sudden-
ness of his departure. Both of us avoided
speaking of the dog, each fearing that his
own experience with the unlucky acquaintance might follow that of our two companions. Tyck, I knew, was more subject to
colds than the rest of us, for he had never
been completely acclimated in Flanders, and
he doubtless feared that one of the frequent
slight attacks that troubled him might prove
at last as serious as the illness that now
threatened poor Henley. With Henley's
departure Antwerp would lose half its attraction for us, for since the death of old
Reiner we three had been even more closely
attached than before. Henley had lost some
of his insular coldness and formality of manner, was daily assuming more and more
the appearance and acquiring the free and
easy habits of an art-student, and his un-
changing good-nature, his stability of character, and his entertaining conversation made
him the leader of our trio. During the ex-
hausting months of the *concours*, and in face

of the discouraging results of weeks of most
energetic and nervous toil, he never lost his
patience, but encouraged us by his superior
strength of purpose and scorn of minor disappointments.

The next day we three met on board the
Baron Osy just before the cables were cast
off the quay. Henley was one of the last
passengers to get aboard, and fortunately our
parting was by necessity short. He was very
weak, and evidently failed from hour to hour,
for he could walk only with the support of
his brother's arm. He said good-by hopelessly but calmly, and we parted with scarcely
another word. We felt that regrets were useless and words of encouragement vain, and
that the only thing that remained to do was
to accept his fate calmly, and as calmly await
our own. There was not a shadow of hope
that we would ever meet again, and I can
never forget the far-off look in Henley's face
as he turned his eyes for an instant towards
the swift, yellow current of the Scheldt, with
the rich-hued sails, the fleecy spring clouds,
and the gorgeously colored roofs of Saint

Anneke reflected in its eddying surface. The cables were cast off and we hurried ashore. In the bustle and confusion a black poodle was driven off the plank by one of the stewards, but the crowd was so great and the noise and the tumult of the wharf-men so distracting, that it was impossible to see whether the dog remained on the boat or was put ashore. However, we saw him no more, and did not doubt that he went with Henley to London. In less than two weeks a letter from Henley's brother announced the death of our friend from quick consumption. Nothing was said of the dog.

From that time Tyck was preoccupied; he was much alone, ceased to frequent the academy, and neither worked nor diverted himself: it was plain that he needed change. Antwerp, at the best a cheerless town, gay on the surface, perhaps, because its people are as thoughtless and improvident as children, but full of misery and well-concealed wretchedness, grew hateful to us both.

Suddenly Tyck announced his purpose of going to Italy, and I resolved to break my

camp as well, make an artistic tour of the
East, and meet my friend in Rome in the
autumn. We divided our canvases and easels
among the rest of the fellows, rolled up our
studies, and with the color-box, knapsack,
and travelling-rug were prepared in a day to
leave the scene of our sad experiences. It
was with feelings of great relief and satisfaction that we saw the red roofs of Antwerp disappear behind the fortifications as
the train carried us southward.

II.

Eight months after Tyck and I parted at
Brussels, I arrived in Rome. Sharing, as I
did, the general ignorance in regard to the
severity of the Italian winters, I was surprised
to find the weather bitterly cold. It was
the day before Christmas, and a breeze that
would chill the bones swept the deserted
streets. After three months' idling in the
East, paddling in the Golden Horn, dream-
ily watching from the hills of Smyrna the
far-off islands of the Grecian Archipelago,

and sleeping in the sun on the rocks at Piræus, Italy seemed as cold and barren as the shores of Scandinavia. It is a popular mistake to winter in Italy. The West of England, the South of France, and many sections of our own country are far preferable. It is not to be denied that Italy can be thoroughly enjoyed only in the warm months. Even 'n the hottest season, Americans find Naples, Rome, and Florence less uncomfortable than Boston, New York, and Philadelphia. Immediately on my arrival Tyck came to meet me at the hotel, and we spent a happy Christmas Eve, discussing the thousand topics that arise when two intimate friends meet after a separation like our own. Tyck was in better health and spirits than I had ever known him to be in before, and to all appearances Italian air agreed with him. In the course of the evening he gave me an invitation to make one of a breakfast-party that was to celebrate Christmas in his studio the next day, and the invitation was accompanied with the request to bring eatables and liquids enough to satisfy my own appe-

tite on that occasion—a Bohemian fashion of
giving dinner-parties to which we were no
strangers.   Accordingly, the next morning
at eleven o'clock we were to meet again in
Tyck's quarters.

The studio was in the fifth story of a large
block not far from the Porta del Popolo, and
looked out upon a large portion of the city,
the view embracing the Pincio and St. Pe-
ter's, Monte Mario, and the Quirinal.   The
entrance on the street was dismal and prison-
like.   A long, dark corridor led back to a
small court at the bottom of a great pit
formed by the walls of the crowded houses,
and the stones of the pavement were flood-
ed with the drippings from the buckets of
all the neighborhood, as they slid up and
down the wire guys leading into the antique
well in one corner, and rattled and splashed
until they were drawn up by an unseen hand
far above in the maze of windows and balco-
nies—an ingenious and simple way of drawing water, quite common in Rome.   From
this sunless court-yard a broad, musty staircase twisted and turned capriciously up past

narrow, gloomy passages to the upper floors
of the house. At the fourth story began a
narrow wooden staircase, always perfumed
with the odors of the adjacent kitchens;
and it grew narrower and steeper and more
crooked until it met a little dark door at the
very top, bearing the name of Tyck. The
suite of rooms which Tyck occupied made
up one of those mushroom-like wooden
stories that are lightly stuck on the top of
substantial stone or brick buildings. They
add to the beauty of the silhouette, but detract from the dignity of the architectural
effect, and look like the cabin of a wrecked
ship flung upon the rocks. From the outside, quaint little windows, pretty hanging
gardens, or an airy *loggia* make the place
look cheerful and cosy. Within, one feels
quite away from the world; far up beyond
neighbors and enclosing walls, tossed on a
sea of roofs, and with a broad sweep of the
horizon on every side. Such a perch is as attractive as it is difficult to reach, and offers
to the artist the advantages of light, quiet,
and perfect freedom. Tyck's rooms were

three in number. A narrow corridor led past
the door of the store-room to the studio—a
large, square room with a great window on
the north side and smaller ones with shutters on the east and west.   From the studio
a door opened into the chamber, in turn
connected with the store-room.   Thus there
was a public and a private entrance to the
studio.

The Christmas breakfast had more than
ordinary significance: it was to be the occasion of the presentation of Tyck's household
to his artist friends.   This, perhaps, needs
explanation.   At the time of our departure
from Antwerp, Tyck was engaged to be
married to a young lady, the daughter of a
Flemish merchant, and there was every prospect of a wedding within a year.   After he
had been absent two or three months her letters ceased to come, and Tyck learned from a
friend that the thrifty father of the girl had
found a match more desirable from a mer-
cenary point of view, and had obliged his
daughter to break engagement number one
in order to enter into a new relation.   Tyck,

after some months of despondency, at last
made an alliance with a Jewish girl of the
working class, and it was at the Christmas
breakfast that Lisa was to be presented for
the first time to the rest of the circle. When
I entered the studio there were already a
good many fellows present. The apartment was a picture in itself; and a long din-
ing-table placed diagonally across the room,
bearing piles of crockery and a great *pièce
montée* of evergreen and oranges, and surrounded by a unique and motley assemblage
of chairs, did not detract from the pictu-
resqueness of the interior.

As studios go, this would not, perhaps,
have been considered luxurious or of extraordinary interest, but it had a character of its
own. Two sides of the room were hung with
odd bits of old tapestry and stray squares of
stamped leather, matched together to make
an irregular patchwork harmonious in tone
and beautifully rich in color. In the corner
were bows and arrows, spears, and other
weapons, brought from Java, a branch or
two of palm, and great reeds from the Cam-

pagna with twisted and shrivelled leaves,
yellow and covered with dust. Studies of
heads and small sketches were tucked away
between the bits of tapestry and leather,
and thus every inch of these walls was covered. On another wall was a book-shelf with
a confused pile of pamphlets and paper-cov-
ered books, and under this hung a number
of silk and satin dresses, various bits of rich
drapery, a coat or two, and a Turkish fez.
The remaining wall, and the two narrow
panels on either side of the great window,
were completely covered with studies of tor-
sos, drawings from the nude, academy heads,
sketches of animals and landscapes, together with a shelf of trinkets, a skeleton, and a
plaster death-mask of a friend hung with a
withered laurel-wreath. Quaint old chairs,
bits of gilded stage furniture, racks of port-
folios, a small table or two covered with the
odds and ends of draperies, papers, sketches,
the accumulation of months, filled the corners and spread confusion into the middle
of the room. Three or four easels huddled
together under the light, holding stray pan-

els and canvases and half-finished pictures, a
lay-figure—that stiff and angular caricature
of the human form—and a chair or two loaded with brushes, color-box, and palettes, witnessed that tools were laid aside to give room
for the table that filled every inch of vacant
space.   In one corner was an air-tight stove,
and this was piled up with dishes and surrounded by great tin boxes, whence an appe-
tizing steam issued forth, giving a hint of the
good things awaiting us.   The bottles were
beginning to form a noble array on the table,
and as often as a new guest appeared, a servant with a *porte-manger* and a couple of bottles would contribute to the army of black
necks and add to the breastwork of loaded
dishes that flanked the stove.   Tyck was in
his element, welcoming heartily and with
boyish enthusiasm every arrival, and leading
the shout of joy at the sight of a fat bundle
or a heavy weight of full bottles.   By eleven
o'clock every one was on hand, and there
was an embarrassment of riches in the eat-
ing and drinking line.   Before sitting down
at the table—there were eighteen of us—we

made a rule that each one should in turn act
as waiter and serve with his own hand the
dishes he had brought, the intention being
to divide the accumulated stock of dishes
into a great many different courses. French
was chosen as the language of the day.

While we were discussing the question of
language, Lisa came in and was presented to
us all in turn, impressing us very favorably.
She was slight, but not thin, with dark hair,
large brown eyes, and a transparent pink-and-
white complexion—a fine type of a Jewess.
She took the place of honor at Tyck's right
hand, and we sat down in a very jolly mood.

The *menu* of that breakfast would craze
a French cook, and the arrangement of the
courses was a work of great difficulty, involv-
ing much general discussion. The *trattorie*
of Rome had been ransacked for curious and
characteristic national dishes; every combination of goodies that ingenious minds could
suggest was brought, and plain substantials
by no means failed. In the *hors d'œuvre*,
we had excellent fresh caviare, the contri-
bution of a Russian; Bologna sausage and

nibbles of radish; and, to finish, *pâté de foie gras*. Soup *à la jardinière* was announced, and was almost a failure at the start-off, because one very important aid to the enjoyment of soup, the spoons, had been forgotten by the contributor. A long discussion as to the practicability of leaving the soup to the end of the meal, meanwhile ordering spoons to be brought, terminated in the employment of extra glasses in place of spoons and soup-plates. Then all varieties of fish followed in a rapid succession of small courses. Tiny minnows fried in delicious olive-oil; crabs and crawfish cooked in various ways; Italian oysters, small, thin, and coppery in flavor; canned salmon from the Columbia River; *baccalà* and herrings from the North Sea; broad, gristly flaps from the body of the devil-fish, the warty feelers purple and suggestive of the stain of sepia and of Victor Hugo—all these, and an abundance of each, were passed around. An immense joint of roast beef, with potatoes, contributed by an Englishman; a leg of mutton, by a Scotchman; a roast pig, from a

Hungarian; the potted meat of Australia, and the tasteless *manzo* of Italy, formed the solid course. Next we devoured a whole flock of juicy larks with crisp skins, pigeons in pairs, ducks from the delta of the Tiber, a turkey brought by an American, pheasants from a Milanese, squash stuffed with meat and spices, and a globe of *polenta* from a Venetian. At this point in the feast there were cries of quarter, but none was given. An English plum-pudding of the unhealthiest species, with flaming sauce; a pie or two strangely warped and burned in places, from the ignorance of the Italian cook or the bad oven; pots of jelly and marmalade, fruit mustard, stewed pears, and roasted chestnuts, *ekmekataïf* and *havláh* from a Greek, a profusion of fruits of all kinds, were offered, and at last coffee was served to put in a paragraph. The delicate wines of Frascati and Marino, the light and dark Falernian, a bottle of Tokay, one of Vöslau, thick red wine of Corfu, and flasks of the ordinary Roman mixture —a little more than water, a little less than wine—Capri *rosso* and *bianco*, Bordeaux and

Burgundy, good English ale and porter, Vienna beer, American whiskey, and Dutch gin, Alkermes, Chartreuse, and Greek mastic, made, all told, a wine-list for a king, and presented a rank of arguments to convert a prohibitionist. This was no orgy that I am describing, simply a jolly breakfast for eighteen Bohemians of all nationalities—a complex, irregular affair, but for that reason all the more delightful.

When we, were well along in the bill of fare, a little incident occurred which put me out of the mood for further enjoyment of the breakfast, and for the rest of the day my position was that of silent spectator, watching the amusements with an expression not calculated to encourage sport. To begin with, I was unusually sensitive to nervous shocks, from the fact that my first impression of Rome had been intensely disagreeable. I found myself in a strangely exciting atmosphere, and subject to unpleasant influences. The first night passed in Rome was crowded with visions, and I cannot recall a period of twenty-four hours during

my residence in that city that has not its
unpleasant souvenir of strange hallucinations, wonderful dreams, or some shock to
my nerves. The meeting with Tyck was
doubtless the occasion of my visions and
restlessness on the night before the Bohemian breakfast. The events of the previous
winter in Antwerp came freshly to my
mind; I lived over again that dark season
of horrors, and the atmosphere of Rome
nourished the growth of similar strange
fancies. There was, however, in my train
of thoughts on Christmas Eve no forebod-
ing that I can recall, no prophetic fear of a
continuance of the strange relations with
that black poodle which had already taken
away the best half of our circle. It needed
little, nevertheless, to put me in a state of
mind very similar to that which tortured me
for months in Antwerp.

But to return to the breakfast. While
we were at the table a hired singer and
guitar-player, a young girl of sixteen or
seventeen years, sang Italian popular songs
and performed instrumental pieces. She
   16

had nearly exhausted her list when she began to sing the weird, mournful song of
Naples, "Palomella," at that time quite the
rage, but since worn threadbare, and its
naïve angles and depressions polished down
to the meaningless monotony of a popular
ditty. We heard a dog howl in the sleeping-
room as the singer finished the ballad, and
Lisa rose to open the door. My seat on
Tyck's left brought me quite near the door,
and I turned on my chair to watch the entrance of the animal. A black poodle, as
near as I could judge the exact counterpart
of the Flemish dog, quietly walked into the
room, evidently perfectly at home. My
first calm reflection was that it was an hallucination, a mental reproduction of one
of the grim pictures of the past winter; I
could not believe my own vision, and it was
some time before I came to realize the fact
that my senses were not deceived. I was
about to ask Tyck if he had noticed in the
dog any curious resemblance to our self-
appointed companion in Antwerp, when he
turned, and, as I thought then, with a lin-

gering touch of the old superstitious fear in
his voice, said: "You've noticed the dog;
he belongs to Lisa. When he first came
here, a month ago, I was horrified to find in
him the image of our Flemish friend. Lisa
laughed me out of my fears, saying that
the animal had been in the family for six
months or more, and at last I began to
look upon him as a harmless pup, and to
wonder only at the strange coincidence."
But I could not turn the affair into a joke
or forget for a moment past events, now
recalled so vividly to my mind. This was
the third time that a black poodle had
taken a liking to one of us, and two out
of the three attachments had already
proved fatal to the human partner. It was
not by any means clear that the same dog
played these different renderings of one
part, but to all appearance it was the
identical poodle. If in two cases this
friendship of the dog for his self-chosen
master had proved fatal, it was but a natural inference that the third attachment
would terminate in a similar manner. But

Tyck was in better health than ever before, notwithstanding the companionship of the dog. Was not this a proof of the folly of my superstition? I asked myself. Reasons were not wanting to disprove the soundness of my logic. It was undoubtedly true that stranger and more wonderful coincidences had happened, and nothing had come of them, and it was undeniable that the imagination might distort facts to such a degree that coincidences would be suspected where none existed. If it were only a coincidence, fears were childish. And the dog manifested no particular friendship for Tyck; he belonged to Lisa, and seemed to take no special notice of any one else.

The *déjeuner* went on without further interruption, and the guitar girl drummed away until the table was cleared. We were not at a loss for entertainments after the feast was ended. Tyck's costumes were drawn upon, and a Flemish musician sang a costume duet with a Walloon sculptor, one being laced up in a blue satin ball-dress, and the other stag-

gering under the weight of a janissary's
uniform. Later on there was a dancing *con-*
cours, in which the Indian war-dance, the
English jig, the negro walk-around, the tar-
antella, the Flemish *reuske*, and the Hungarian *csárdás* each had its nimble-footed
performers. The scene was worth putting
upon canvas. The confusion of quaint and
rare trinkets, the abundance of color-bits,
and the picturesque groups of figures in
all the costumes that could be improvised
for the dance or the song—a museum of
bric-à-brac and a carnival of characters—all
this made a *tableau vivant* of great richness
and interest.

About the middle of the afternoon the
entertainment began to flag a little, and the
moment there was a lull in the sport some
one proposed a trip to Ponte Molle. The
vote was immediately taken and carried, and
we marched out to the Piazza del Popolo
and engaged an omnibus for the rest of the
day.

The straggling suburb outside the Porta
del Popolo was lively with pleasure-seeking

Romans. The wine-shops were full of sad-eyed peasants and weary, careworn laborers; all the mournful character of a Roman merry-making was unusually prominent on this cheerless holiday, and the cloaked natives chatted as solemnly as if they were mourners at a funeral. Roman festivities are, in general, not calculated to divert the participants to a dangerous extent. Wine-drinking is the chief amusement; and even under the enlivening influences of his potations the Roman rarely loses his habitual seriousness of manner, but bears himself to the end of the orgy as if he expected every moment to be called upon to answer for the sins of his ancestors. As we drove along the straight, broad road that raw afternoon, we met numberless carts and omnibuses filled with laborers returning from the wine-shops in the Campagna; the sidewalks were crowded with people on their way to and from the *trattorie* near the Tiber; and scarcely a song was heard, rarely a laugh sounded above the rattle of the wheels. The natives were making a business of amusement, and formed a staid

and sober procession, on an occasion when in
Germany or Belgium the frolics and noisy mer-
riment of the people would have known no
bounds short of the limit of physical endur-
ance. We were probably regarded as escaped
maniacs because we persisted in breaking
the voiceless confusion by our hearty Flemish songs. We left the omnibus in the yard
of a *trattoria* at some distance out in the Campagna, and strolled over the hills for an hour,
watching the dark, cold mountains and the
broad, sad-tinted waste spread out before us.
The solemn beauty of the Campagna is always impressive; under a gray sky it as-
sumes a sombre and mournful aspect. To
the north of the city the low, flat-topped
hills combine in a peculiar way to form sil-
houettes of great nobleness of character and
simplicity of line. They are the changeless
forms that endure like the granite cliffs,
monumental in their grandeur. When
moving shadows of the clouds form purple patches across these hills, and the dull
gray of the turf comes into occasional relief in a spot of strong sunlight, the scene is

one of unique and matchless beauty — a
heroic landscape, with wonderful vigor and
dignity of line and extraordinary delicacy of
tone. That afternoon the dog, which had
accompanied Tyck on the excursion, furnished us our chief amusement. We tossed
sticks down the steep gravel banks, to watch
his lithe black form struggle through the
brambles, seize the bit, and return it to us.
He, poor animal, had probably been shut up
within the walls of Rome longer than the
rest of the party, and entered into the out-
door frolics with even more zest than his
human companions. Below the *trattoria*
there was a narrow brook bridged by a rail,
and we tried to get the poodle to walk this
narrow path, but with no success. Tyck at
last made the attempt, to encourage the
dog, but on his way back he slipped and wet
his feet and ankles thoroughly. Most of us
thought this accident of not the least importance, but one or two of the old residents advised a return to the wine-shop, hinting of
a possible serious illness in consequence of
the wetting. At the *trattoria* Tyck dried

himself at the large open fire in the kitchen,
and we thought no more of it. The old
Porta del Popolo answered our chorus with
a welcoming echo as we drove in, shortly
after dark, and mingled with the shivering
crowd hurrying to their homes. Our Christmas had at least been a merry one to the
most of us, but I could not forget the incident of the dog; and as I walked through
the streets to my cheerless room a strange
dread gradually took entire possession of me
in spite of my reason.

For a day or two, that least amusing of
all occupations, studio-hunting, kept me
busy from morning till night, and I saw
none of the breakfast-party. It was beginning to surprise me that Tyck did not make
his appearance, when I had a call from
Lisa, bearing a message from him, saying he
was slightly unwell and wanted me to come
and see him. I lost no time in complying
with his request. On my way to his room
the same old dread, stifled for a while in the
busy search for rooms, came back with all
its force, and I already began to suffer the

first agonies of grief at the loss of my friend. For, although the message was hopeful enough, it came at a time when it seemed the first sign of the fulfilment of my forebodings, and from that moment I looked upon Tyck as lost to us. Not pretending to myself that it was an excusable weakness on my part to become the victim of what would generally be declared a morbid state of the imagination; reasoning all the while that the weather, the peculiar, tomb-like atmosphere of Rome, our previous experience in Antwerp, and our long absence from the distractions and worldliness of a civilized society would have caused this state of mind in healthier organizations than my own; I still could not help thinking of my friend as already in the clutch of death, and soon to be numbered as the third lost from our little circle, while the fourth was still to wait.

Tyck was in bed when I entered his chamber. There was a fresh glow deep in his brown cheek, and his eyes seemed to me brighter than usual; still there was no visible sign of a dangerous illness, and my rea-

son laughed at my fears.   He complained of
dizziness, headache, pains in the back, and
coughed at intervals.   His manner showed
that his mind was troubled, and from Lisa
I learned that he had not yet received the
expected remittance for the sale of his
last pictures sent to London.   The winter
was severe and fuel expensive ; models were
awaiting payment, and the rent-day was
drawing near.   I gave Lisa all the money I
had with me, and charged her to keep me
posted as to the wants of the household, if
by any bad fortune Tyck should be obliged
to keep his room for any length of time.   She
afterwards told me that later in the day several friends called, suspected the state of
affairs, and each contributed according to his
purse—always without the knowledge of the
sufferer.

Every day after that, I passed a portion
of the daylight in Tyck's room.   His cough
gradually grew more violent, and in a day or
two he became seriously ill with high fever.
The doctor, a spare, wise-looking German, of
considerable reputation as a successful practi-

tioner in fever cases, was called that day and afterwards made more frequent visits than the length of our purses would warrant.   On the third or fourth day he decided that the disease was typhoid fever, and commenced a severe and to us inexperienced nurses a harsh treatment, dosing continually with quinine and blistering the extremities.   Before the end of a week Tyck fell into long spells of delirium, and recognized his friends only at intervals.   His tongue was black, and protruded from his mouth, and between his fits of coughing he could at last only whisper a few words in Italian.   We had been in the habit of conversing at discretion in English, French, Flemish, or German; talking always on art questions in French, telling stories in the picturesque Flemish patois, and reserving the German and English languages for more solemn conversation. Tyck would frequently attempt to use one of these languages when he wished to speak with me during his illness, aware of my slight acquaintance with Italian, and it was most painful to witness his struggles

with an English or French sentence. The
words seemed too rasping for his tender
throat and blistered tongue; the easy enun-
ciation of the Italian vowels gave him no
pain, and in a sigh he could whisper a whole
sentence.

When at last Lisa was quite worn out
with nursing, and there was need of more
skilful and experienced hands to adminis-
ter the medicines and perform the thousand
duties of a sick-room, the doctor advised us
to make application at a convent for a sister
to come and watch at night. We did so,
and on the evening of the same day a cheerful, home-like little body, in the stiffest of
winged bonnets, climbed the long stairs and
took immediate possession of the sick-room,
putting things into faultless order in a very
few moments. Her first step was to banish
the dog to a neighboring studio, and I awaited her entrance into the painting-room with
some anxiety. The long table had been re-
moved, but otherwise the studio remained
just the same as it was on the day of the
feast. A regiment of bottles was drawn up

near the window; various tell-tale dishes,
broken glasses, and other *débris* cluttered
the corner near where the stove stood, and
I was sure that a lecture on the sin of the
debauchery which had brought my friend
to a sick-bed awaited me the moment the
sister saw these proofs of our worldliness.
She trotted out into the studio at last, in
the course of her busy preparation for the
night; and then, instead of bursting forth
with a reproof, she covered her face with
her hands, turned about, and walked out of
the house. I, of course, followed her and
begged for an explanation. She hesitated
long, but finally with some difficulty said
she could not stay in a room where such
pictures decorated the walls, and before she
would consent to return she must be assured
of their removal or concealment. I hastened
up, covered all the academy studies with bits
of newspaper; and the sister returned and
went on with her duties as if nothing had
happened. So the expected lecture was
never delivered. In the sight of the greater
enormity of academy studies, she clearly

thought it useless to lecture on the appetite.

Few days elapsed after the sister took charge of the sick-room before we were all rejoiced at an improvement in Tyck. He grew better rapidly, and in two weeks was able to sit up in bed and talk to us. Though we were full of joy at his apparent speedy recovery, there was always a bitterness in the thought that the fatal relapse might be expected at every moment, and this shadow hung over us even in the most hopeful hours. The sister gave up her charge, and as Tyck grew better day by day, Lisa came to act as sole nurse and companion, although we made daily visits to the sick-room. The month of January passed, and Carnival approached. Tyck was able to have his clothes put on, and to move around the room a little. The doctor made infrequent and irregular visits, and but for the fear of a relapse would have ceased to come altogether.

The morning of the first day of Carnival week, I was awakened while it was still dark by the ringing of my door-bell, and lay in bed for a while undecided whether it was not a dream that had roused me. My studio and apartment were of a very bogyish character, located at the top of a house on the Tiber, completely shut away from the world, and full of dream - compelling influences that lurked in the dingy and long-disused bedroom with its worn and faded furniture, and filled the spacious studio and the musty little *salon* with an oppressive presence, which did not vanish in the brightest days nor in the midst of the liveliest assembly that ever gathered there. So it never astonished me to be awakened by some unaccountable noise, or by the mental conviction that there was some disturbance in the crowded atmosphere. When I was aroused that dark, drizzly morning, I awaited the second pull of the bell before I summoned courage enough to pass through the shadowy *salon* and the lofty studio, with its ghostly lay-figure and plaster casts, like pale phantoms in the dim light of a wax taper, and open the great door that led into the

narrow corridor. A slender form wrapped
in a shawl entered the studio, and Lisa stood
there, pale with fright, her great brown eyes
drowned in tears, shrinking from the invisible terrors that seemed to pursue her. She
whispered that Tyck was worse, and asked
me to go for the doctor. I led her back to
Tyck's room, and in an hour the doctor was
there.

The details of that last illness are painful
in the extreme. The sister was not in attend-
ance, it having been decided by the superior
that artists' studios were places whither the
duties (˙ the sisterhood did not call its members, and so Lisa's mother came and did her
best to fill, in a rough sort of way, the delicate
office of nurse. On the last day of Carnival,
little suspecting that the end of my friend
was near, I was occupied in my own studio
until nearly dark, and just as the sport was at
its height I struggled through the crowd and
reached Tyck's studio, white with *confetti*
and flour, and in a state of mind hardly
fitted for the sick-room. In the studio
two doctors sat in consultation, and their

17

serious faces, with the frightened look in
Lisa's eyes, told me the sad story at once.
They had decided that Tyck must die, and
made a last examination just after I entered.
They raised him in bed, thumped his poor
back, pulled out his swollen tongue, and felt
of his tender scalp, burned with fever and
frozen with a sack of ice. The group at
the bedside, so picturesquely impressive, will
always remain in my memory like the souvenir of some gloomy old picture. Lisa's
mother was seated on the back of the bed,
raising Tyck like a sick child, his limp arms
dangling over her shoulders and his head
drooping against her cheek. To the right
the slight and graceful form of Lisa, holding
the earthen lamp; one doctor bending over
to listen at the bared back, the focus of
the dim light; the other doctor solemn and
motionless, a dark silhouette against the
bed and the wall beyond. The examination
only proved the truth of the decision just
reached, and it was then announced for the
first time that the real malady was lung-
fever, with the not infrequently accompany-

ing first symptoms of typhoid. A few moments later one or two young artists dropped in, learned the sad news, and went away to warn the rest of the friends. At eight o'clock we were all in the studio, and after a hushed and hasty discussion as to whether or not a priest should be called in this last hour, the Catholic friends were overruled, and it was decided to consult no spiritual adviser. Tyck, meanwhile, was scarcely able to talk. One by one the fellows came to his bedside, were recognized, and went away. I alone stayed in the studio, waiting, waiting. The doctor was to come at half-past nine, and the fellows had promised to return again at ten.

For a long hour we sat in silence, Lisa and I, and watched the approach of death. The mother, completely exhausted, lay on the bare floor near the stove, as motionless as a corpse; the dim light reflected from the sick-room transformed the draperies into mysterious shapes, and made the lay-figure look vaporous and spectral. Frequent fits of violent, suffocating cough would call us to the bedside, and after a severe struggle Tyck would for a moment throw off the clutch of the malady and breathe again. He was in agony to speak with me, but was unable to. I guessed part of his wishes, repeated them in Flemish, and he made a signal of assent when I was right. In this way he communicated certain directions about his affairs, and I promised to see Lisa provided for and all his business properly settled. But there was something more he was anxious to tell, and he continued to the last his vain struggle to express it.

The stillness of the studio in the intervals between the spasms of suffocation was painfully broken, as the long hour passed, by his heavy breathing and by the stifled sobs of the poor girl, who, at last, cried herself to sleep, exhausted by her watching. From outside, a dog's mournful howl, breaking into a short, spasmodic bark, came up at intervals, and I could see that this sound disturbed the sufferer, probably recalling to his waning faculties the history of the dog that had so haunted us. From the street the

chorus of the maskers came floating to us,
sounding hollow and far away, like the chant
of a distant choir in some great cathedral.
Occasionally a carriage rumbled over the
rough pavement, the deep sound echoing
through the deserted court-yard and up the
long, dreary stairways. It was within a few
moments of the doctor's expected visit that
a spasm more violent than any previous one
called me to the bedside. We had long
since stopped the medicine, and nothing remained to do but to ease the sufferer over
the chasm as gently as possible. He did not
seem at all anxious to live, and in the
agonies of the suffocation there was no fear
in those dark eyes that rolled in their hollow
sockets. I raised him in bed, and at last,
after the most prolonged fight, he caught his
breath, opened his eyes, turned towards me,
and said plainly in English, " All right, old
boy." Then he relapsed into a comatose
state and never spoke again. The doctor
found him rapidly sinking, and another
spasm came on while he was feeling the
pulse. The patient recovered from it only

to pass into another and more protracted one, at the end of which he sighed twice and was dead. For a second or two after the last deep breath his face had all the fever-flush and the look of life, but almost instantly he fell over towards me, changed beyond recognition. The wave of death had passed over us, carrying with it the last trace of life that lingered in the face of my friend, and a ghastly pallor crept over his cheeks, transforming him that I loved into an unrecognizable, inert thing. I turned away and never saw that face again, although they told me it was nobly beautiful in its Egyptian, changeless expression. That pause of an instant, while death was asserting its power, impressed me strangely— and this was no new experience for me. In that pause, when time seemed to stand still, something urged me to raise my eyes in confident expectation of seeing the spirit as it left the body. Even my heated imagination, to which I was ready to charge much that was inexplicable in my experience, did not produce an image, but

instead, where the wall should have been I
seemed to look into space, into a wide, wide
distance.   An awful vacancy, an infinity of
emptiness, yawned before me, and I looked
down to meet the fixed expression of that
changed face.   For that moment there was
no lingering presence of my friend that I
could feel; in that short struggle he had
separated himself entirely from us and from
the place he used to fill with his charming presence.   In the chamber of death
there was no adumbration of the life that
once flourished there, of the soul that
had just fled.   And so I thought only of
burying the body and providing for poor
Lisa.

The rest of the fellow-painters came a few
moments after it was all over, and received
the news with surprise.   Lisa still slept, and
we did not wake her.   I remained in the
studio all night, and in the morning the for-
malities of the police notification were gone
through with, and the preparations made for
the funeral.   In the studio, unchanged in
every respect from the day when Tyck put

his brushes in his palette and laid it upon a chair, we held a meeting to decide upon the funeral ceremonies. Lisa was completely broken down by grief and exhaustion, and, with her mother and the dog, who joyfully occupied his old place by the stove and disputed the entrance of every one, lived in the studio and the store-room.

On Sunday morning we buried our friend in the Protestant cemetery. Arriving at the little house in the enclosure, we found the coffin there, with the undertaker, Lisa, her mother, and the dog. An hour later an English minister came and conducted the ceremonies in a cold, hurried manner; but perhaps the services were quite as satisfactory, after all, because his language was unintelligible to the majority of those present. We stood shivering in a circle around the coffin until the services were over, and then bore the burden to the grave, dug deep near the wall in a picturesque nook under a ruined tower—a fit monument to our friend. Lisa and her mother stood a little apart, holding the dog, while we put the body in the grave, and a cold sun shone down upon us, quite as cheerless and as unsympathetic as the dull, lowering clouds of that day in Flanders a year before. After the customary handful of earth had been thrown, we turned away and separated, for the living had no sympathy with each other after the cold formality of the funeral. As I strolled across the field in the direction of Monte Testaccio, I looked back once only. There, on the mound of fresh earth, stood the dog, and Lisa was bending over to arrange a wreath of immortelles.

After the sale of Tyck's effects, which brought a comfortable little sum to Lisa, I left Rome, now unbearable, and sought the distractions of busy Naples. Later, with warm weather, I settled in a solitary nest in Venice, where the waves of the lagoon lapped my door-step. The distressed cries of a dog called me to the water door, one rainy morning, while I was writing a part of this very narrative, and I pulled out of the water a half-drowned, shaggy black dog. With some anxiety I assisted the poor animal to dry his fur, and found, instead of my old enemy, a harmless shaggy terrier, who rests his dainty nose on the paper as I write.

And so the fourth still waits.

THE BUSH

THE BUSH

THE six short stories in this volume have all been written at sea in those brief intervals of enforced rest from an exacting profession which a transatlantic voyage compels; and I have offered them to the public with the full knowledge of the necessity of some explanation to palliate my offence of meddling with literature, and in the belief that I must hang out some sort of a bush to call attention to whatever merits they may have. This bush will be a confession, made, like the confidential communications in all prefaces, into the ear of the reader alone. The reason why I have put my preface—if I may be permitted to misuse the term—at the end of the book instead of at the beginning, is that the confidences I impart may be, by reason of their position between the covers, less likely to be read by the careless or mechanical reviewer or by the superficial " skimmer " of fiction. I was afraid that if the reader should by chance read the preface first, he would not care to peruse the stories, because, having been admitted to the dark room, as it were, and having had the formula of the developer told to him, he might, after he had seen one set of images come up on the dull surface of the negative, find his curiosity abated, his interest gone, and his desire satisfied.

These stories have been published in various magazines, at different times, since the centennial year. When the earliest one of the series appeared, I was not a little flattered by being often asked how much of it was true. When the second one came out, this question grew a little stale, and I began to resent the curiosity as to my method of story-telling. The climax was finally reached when I received a letter from a writer of most excellent short stories, in which communication he desired information about the characters in the tale, and led me to understand that he believed the main part of the tale to be true. In my answer to his letter I wrote him this old story of the Western bar-room: A crowd of men were leaning over a bar drinking together and listening to the yarns of a frontiersman who, stimulated by the laughter and applause, was drawing a very long bow. His triumph was not quite complete, however, for he noticed a thin, silent man at the farther end of the bar, whose face did not change its habitual expression at any of the mirth- or wonder-compelling incidents. At last, having directed the fire of his dramatic expression for some time towards the silent man with no result, the Western Munchausen turned to him with an oath and said: "Why in —— don't you laugh or cry, or do something, when I tell a story?" "The fact is, stranger," the sad man replied, in a mournful tone of voice—"the fact is, I'm a liar myself!" I never heard from my correspondent again.

We all think we have fertile imaginations, and no one can blame me for not liking to be denied the credit of invention and imagination, even if the stories be mostly true. It seemed to me quite as foolish to expect a short story to be a simple chronicle of some experience with changed names and localities as it would be to demand of an historical artist that he paint only those events of history of which he has been an actual spectator. However, while this suspicion of the existence of a foundation of truth was not altogether flattering or encouraging, it did set me to thinking what part of these stories was actually drawn from my real experience, in what way the ideas arose, grew, and developed into stories. The result of this examination—the confession of the proportion of truth to fiction—is the bush, then, which I propose to hang out.

The plot of the " Capillary Crime " turns on the force of capillary attraction in wood. The remote origin of the idea was reading about the employment of wooden wedges in ancient quarries, which were first driven in dry and then, on being wetted, swelled and burst off the blocks of stone. While living in Paris, in the Rue de l'Orient, a small street on Montmartre, which was lighted at that time by lanterns hung on ropes across from house to house, I had occasion to take out the breech-pin of an old Turkish flint-lock gun in order to draw the charge. It was impossible to start the plug at first, but after it had been soaked for a short time in petroleum it was easily unscrewed. Capillary attraction had carried the oil into the rusted threads of the screw. The knowledge of this action, together with the memory of the immense power of wooden wedges, naturally brought to my mind a possible case where the wetting of wood in a gun-stock might so affect the mechanism of the lock that the hammer would fall without the agency of the trigger. I constructed a model on the plan of the finger of a manikin, and it worked perfectly. An artist in the neighborhood committed suicide just about this time. My studio on Montmartre had once been the scene of a similar tragedy. There was every reason, then, why I selected that studio as the scene; there was a plausible excuse for connecting capillary force with the dis-

18

charge of a gun; there was my recent experience with suicide to warrant a realistic description of such an event. My story was ready-made. I had only to sew together the patchwork pieces.

While I was engaged in revising "A Capillary Crime" for publication in book form, a friend sent me a slip cut from a Western newspaper, which testifies in such an unexpected manner to the possibility of the combination of circumstances described in my story that I insert it here:

"FACT AGAINST FICTION.

"A STRIKING INSTANCE OF THE UNRELIABILITY OF CIRCUMSTANTIAL EVIDENCE.

"There is no figment of the imagination—if it is at all within the limit of possibilities—more curious or strange than some things that actually happen. The following is an instance in proof of this:

"A few years ago Frank Millet, the well-known artist, war correspondent, and story-writer, published a short story in a leading magazine which had as its principal features the mysterious killing of a Parisian artist in his own studio. A web of circumstantial evidence led to the arrest of a model who had been in the habit of posing for him. But through some chain of circumstances which the writer of this has now forgotten, the murder—if murder it can be called—was found to have been caused by the discharge of a firearm through the force of capillary attraction. The firearm was used by the artist as a studio accessory, and was hung in such a manner that he was directly in line with it. Its discharge occurred when he was alone in his studio.

" The story was a vivid and ingenious flight of the imagination. Now for its parallel in fact :

" A recent number of the Albany *Law Journal* tells of the arrest of a man upon the charge of killing his cousin. The dead man was found lying upon a lounge, about three o'clock in the afternoon, with a 32-caliber ball in his brain. The cousin, who had an interest of $100,000 in his death, was alone with him in the house at the time. The discovery of the real cause of death was due to the lawyer of the accused, who took the rifle from which the ball had been fired, loaded and hung it upon the wall, and then marked the form of a man upon a white sheet and placed it upon the lounge where the man had been found. Then a heavy cut-glass pitcher of water was placed upon a shelf above. The temperature was 90° in the shade. The pitcher of water acted as a sun-glass, and the hot rays of the sun shining through the water were refracted directly upon the cartridge chamber of the rifle. Eight witnesses were in the room, and a few minutes after three o'clock there was a puff and a report, and the ball struck the outlined form back of the ear, and the theory of circumstantial evidence was exploded.

"This is interesting, not only because the real occurrence is quite as strange as the imagined one, but because the fact came after the fiction and paralleled it so closely."

I have accurately reported the brief conversation I had with the friend who occupied the Roman studio with me, and can give no further proof of the peculiar character of the place nor add to the description of the uncomfortable sensations we endured there. My friend's remarks so far confirmed my own impressions that I have always felt that he must have had the same experience as myself—if I may call the incident of the simulacrum an experience. He has never to my knowledge talked with any one about this, but now that I have broken the ice in this public manner he may feel called upon to tell his own story, if he has any to relate.

There used to come and pose for me in my Paris studio a Hungarian model who

had been a circus athlete. The ranks of
male models are largely recruited from circus men, actors, lion-tamers—people of all
trades and professions, indeed—and it is not
unusual to find among them individuals of
culture and ability whom some misfortune
or bad habit has reduced to poverty. This
one was an unusually useful model. He had
tattooed on the broad surface of skin over
his left biceps his name, Nagy, not in ordinary letters, but in human figures in different
distorted positions, representing letters of
the alphabet, evidently copied from a child's
cheap picture-book. While I was painting
from him, the war between Russia and Turkey broke out, and the model came one day
and announced that he had joined the Hungarian Legion, and was off for Turkey. As
he left me I said:

"If you're killed, there'll be no trouble in
identifying you, for, unless your left arm is
shot off, you have your passport always with
you."

At that time I had no intention of going
to Turkey myself, but in a few days I found

myself on the way there, and, while passing
through Hungary, Nagy naturally came to
my mind, and it occurred to me that I might
possibly run across him. However, the fortunes of war did not bring us together, and
I never saw him or heard of him again. On
my way through London to America, after
the war, I was witness to a slight trapeze
accident in a circus which, though by no
means startling, recalled to my mind Nagy
and his tattooed name; and then, thinking
over the campaign and meditating on the
possibilities of my having met him there, the
plan of the tale developed itself in a perfectly easy and regular way. I had only to
introduce a little incident of my Italian trav-
els, a bit of local coloring from Turkey, and
the thing was done.

The evolution of " Tedesco's Rubina " was
simpler than that of either of the preceding
stories. Any one familiar with Capri will remember a grotto similar to the one described,
and probably many visitors to that little ter-
restrial paradise have been made acquainted
with the secret of the smugglers' path down

into the grotto. A dozen years or more ago, there was a very old model in Capri who had a remarkable history, and who was accustomed to drone on for hours at a stretch about her early experiences and the artists of a generation or two ago. Sketches of her at different periods of her life hung in most of the public resorts of the island. I made a careful study of this old and wrinkled face, still bearing traces of youthful beauty. The contrast between this painting and the plaster cast of the head of a Roman nymph which occupied a prominent place in my studio was the cause of many a jest, and called forth many a tradition of model life from the garrulous members of that profession. The visible proofs that the old woman had once been the great beauty of the island; the incident of the bust in the museum at Rome; the discovery of human bones in the grotto—all were interwoven together in a web of romance before I even thought of putting it on paper. When I came to write it out, it was very much like telling a threadbare story.

The Latin Quarter in Paris is the most

fertile spot in the world for the growth of romances, most of them of the mushroom species. If a stenographer were to take down the stories he might hear any evening in a *brasserie* there, he would have a unique volume of strange incidents—some of them incredible, perhaps, but all with much flavor of realism about them to make them interesting from a human point of view. Not a few strange suicides, incomprehensible alliances, marvellously curious and pathetic bits of human history, have come under my own notice there. Student life in the Latin Quarter is not all " beer and skittles," for its sordid side is horribly depressing and hopeless. Few who have experienced it have ever entirely recovered from the taint of this unnatural and degrading life.

Away up in the top of one of the largest and most populous hotels of the quarter, an American artist has kept " bachelor hall " for a score of years or more. He is an animal-painter, and spends the winter in elaborating his summer's studies, and in preparing immense canvases for sacrifice before that Jug-

gernaut, the annual Salon. He received once
a commission to paint a portrait—a " post-
mortem," as such a commission is usually
called—of a deceased black-and-tan terrier.
The only data he had to work from were
a small American tintype and the tanned
skin of the defunct pet. Having been inoc-
ulated with the spirit of modern French realism, the artist could not be content with
constructing a portrait of the dog out of the
materials provided, and went to a dog-fancier
and hired an animal as near as could be like
the one in the tintype. At the appointed
hour the dog was brought to the studio in a
covered basket. When the canvas was ready
and the palette set, the artist opened the lid
of the basket and the animal sprang out and
began to run about the room. The artist
thought the dog would soon make himself
at home, so at first he did not attempt to
secure him. But he shortly found that he
grew wilder and more excited every moment,
and that catching him was no easy matter.
After knocking over all the furniture in the
room except the heavy easel, he succeeded

in cornering him and seized him by the col-
lar. A savage bite through the thumb made
him loose his hold, and the rôles of pursuer
and pursued immediately changed. The
beast flew into a terrible state of rage, snap-
ping and snarling like a mad thing. As there
was no safer refuge than the large easel, the
artist climbed upon that to escape his infuri-
ated enemy. By the aid of a long mahl-stock
he fished up the bell-cord which hung within
reach, and pulled it until the concierge came.
The owner of the dog was speedily brought,
and the siege of the studio was raised. The
same artist brought in from the country one
autumn a torpid snake, which he kept in a
box all through the winter. One morning
in spring he was horrified to find the reptile
coiled up on the rug beside his bed. He
killed it by dropping a heavy color-box on it,
without stopping to find out whether it was
venomous or not. It is easy to see how my
story grew out of these two incidents.

Now that the chief actors in the drama which
I have sketched in "The Fourth Waits" are
long since dead, I may confess without fear

of hurting anybody's feelings that all the incidents in this tale are absolutely true. There are plenty of witnesses to the accuracy of this statement, and I have no doubt they would, if called upon, gladly testify to almost every detail of the descriptions. No one who was present at the funeral ceremonies in Antwerp and Rome can ever forget the impression made upon him at the time; neither is any member of the little artistic circle likely to forget to the end of his days the strange sensation of superstitious awe with which the incidents of the story of the stray dog were listened to every time the subject was broached among us. The memory of this experience weighed heavily upon my mind for two or three years, and I only threw off the load after I had written the story.

It is only to complete this series of confessions that I explain how this preface came to be written. I was riding home with a friend late one raw afternoon at the close of a long day's hunting in one of the Midland counties of England, and we stopped to refresh ourselves and horses at a wayside inn called The Holly Bush. When we mounted again at the door, I reached up with my hunting crop and struck the holly bush that hung over the door as a sign. It rattled like metal, and as we rode away I said to my companion:

"That wasn't a real holly bush!"

"That wasn't real whiskey!" he replied.

The memory of the mongoose story which these remarks called up cheered us more than the pause at the inn.

"The mongoose story is almost the only tale that need not be explained even to a Scotchman," my friend added.

This is how I came to think of explaining the construction of my stories, and how I came to call my confessions "The Bush."

THE END.